STORY*GLOSSIA* Fiction Prize 2006

Edited by Steven J. McDermott

Storyglossia Press – Anacortes, WA – 2006

Storyglossia Fiction Prize 2006

Storyglossia Press
1004 Commercial Ave.
#1110
Anacortes WA 98221-4183
www.storyglossia.com/press.html

ISBN: 978-0-6151-3835-0

Printed in the United States of America.

First, edition, first printing: December 2006.

All stories in this collection were previously published, in slightly different form, in Issue 16, October 2006 of the online literary journal STORY*GLOSSIA* (ISSN 1545-2824):

www.storyglossia.com/

STORY*GLOSSIA* Fiction Prize 2006

Winner – **Kristen Tsetsi** for "They Three at Once Were One"

1st Runner-up – **Katrina Denza** for "Snake Dreams"

2nd Runner-up – **Steven Gillis** for "The Society for the Protection of Animals"

3rd Runner-up – **Theresa Boyar** for "Waxing Razal"

Finalists:

Christiana Langenberg for "In-Coming"

Chris Sheehan for "Roots and Limbs"

Gabrielle Idlet for "Vacancies"

Elizabeth Severn for "Dumpster Digging for Daddy"

Bonnie Roop Bowles for "Gizzard Boy"

Hal Ackerman for "Hunting and Fishing"

Congratulations to the prizewinners and the finalists. These stories were originally published in Issue 16, October 2006 of the online literary journal STORY*GLOSSIA*. Interviews with the authors and story analysis by editor Steven J. McDermott can be found at: www.storyglossia.com/fp2006.html

Contents

Kristen Tsetsi

They Three at Once Were One

The news recycled again on the small TV, rabbit-ear antennae half alert, half asleep: A downed helicopter outside of Mosul. A roadside IED. A flipped-over tank in the Euphrates.

Nan checked her phone again for signal bars, then set it beside the plastic plate of Chinese food, uneaten and cold, and lit another cigarette.

A flipped-over tank in the Euphrates.

Just some string of words crossing the Teleprompter, and the anchor even smiled before commercial. "Coming up," she said, "America's obesity crisis." Nan looked past the lobby windows at drifting storm clouds, their depths and flowering expansions revealed in teasing, random lightning flashes. She willed a strike to wipe Marc from her memory—*flash!*—and render him foreign, the way her own language had once sounded foreign when overheard at the fringes of her attention. She had thought it Greek, maybe Italian, until the words came into focus in a wash of air and sound.

Headlights lit the dark lobby, then faded. A new car—a Mustang, yellow, with tinted windows—pulled up under the awning and sat there with the engine running. Nan put out her cigarette, wiped her face with her sleeves, and turned down the TV.

She took her spot behind the counter and noticed mascara on the cuffs of her sleeves. She bunched them in her palms.

The first out of the car was a girl.

Dressed.

Lips red-red. Professionally-styled blonde waves touched her shoulders and Nan knew. They only dressed up like that, got their hair done, for prom, military balls, or for the other. The girl was too old for prom, and not enough military were around for there to be a ball, but Nan still hoped, anyway, that it wouldn't happen today, that it was something else, something—

But it wasn't. Nan saw the hair first—a high-and-tight—before he put on his cap, and then she saw his arms, green-and-brown and gesturing over the car roof.

Nan watched him come around the car, watched the girl step through her held-open glass door. A pressure breeze blew back the girl's hair and she smiled, her lips a narrow red line. He—name patch reading "Tanner"—followed just behind her. He pulled off his cap and held it at his waist.

"Hi," Nan said, and her throat caught. "Help you?" she said, louder.

The girl rested her forearms on the raised counter. Her nails matched her lips, and she wore a tiny round diamond on her left ring finger.

Tanner stuffed his cap in a pocket and put an arm around the girl's lower back. "Babe? It's under your name, isn't it?"

Nan noticed slight movement in his upper arm and imagined his thumb touching the girl's spine.

The girl looked up at Tanner. "Oh. Yes."

He was as tall as Marc. His chin would brush the top of Nan's head, tickle her hair.

"Mackelroy," the girl said. "Jennie." She smiled again.

Nan didn't smile back, but down-arrowed until she found their room. Fifty dollars had been added to the regular rate and the manager's memo read, SOLDIER LEAVE BEGINS.

"Computer error," Nan said. "If you'll wait a moment?" She looked up for an answer.

The girl—Jennie—said, "Sure," and shifted on her feet. Tanner squeezed her close and looked around the lobby, then out at the car. He leaned to whisper something to the girl, and she squeezed his side. "Yeah, but it was your money," she said, nudging him. "All that hazard pay."

"Almost worth it," he said.

Nan smelled—coming from his ACU's—dirt. Dust. The same desert odor that lifted off the pages she'd pulled from sweat-smudged envelopes, fine sand-grain coating her fingertips like chalk powder. She imagined his uniform against her cheek, his breath falling cool on the top of her head. His eyes were shaped like Marc's. The corners, or maybe the—

"Is that a no?" he said.

"Sorry?"

"I said, any good news?" He pointed at the TV.

Nan's face heated. "I—I don't—no. No." She looked at Jennie, who couldn't be much older than nineteen. Too young to not take him for granted. Too naïve to appreciate his standing beside her, his touching and holding and speaking to her. She was picking at her nails, and Nan imagined those nails would later rake silly teenage lines on Tanner's skin. She would write, "I love you" on his back, making love take the shape of a heart.

Before Marc left, Nan had closed her eyes and tried to memorize his body, the lines and bends and moles and wrinkles, with her fingertips.

"Is it not there?" Jennie said.

"Yes. It's just—one moment, please." Nan turned her attention back to the computer and found another room, nicer than their original.

"We're not in any hurry," Tanner said, and Jennie looked at him. "Take your time."

Jennie asked Nan if there was a bathroom and, before leaving, slid her credit card onto the counter. Tanner wandered into Nan's dark lobby and stood with his arms folded on his chest and watched the TV. "Chinese?" he said. He kicked a tan-booted foot in the direction of Nan's table.

She nodded.

"I haven't had Chinese in . . . damn. Too long. Hey, you got the number?"

Nan pointed at the brochure bin. While he looked through fliers, she moved Jennie Mackelroy from room 129 to room 212.

Jennie came out of the bathroom, lipstick refreshed, hair brushed, skin delicately perfumed. Tanner opened his arms and Jennie went into them. He stroked her hair and caught Nan staring.

Nan busied herself with a cup of pens.

Tanner guided Jennie to the counter and picked up the key card and credit card. He said, "Thanks for the delivery stuff," and led Jennie through the door, an arm around her narrow shoulders, pamphlets poking out of a cargo pocket.

Nan pressed her pin-pricked thumb into one of room 129's pillowcases until the blood soaked through. Three days ago, it had been cornflakes softened in milk and splattered in a dark corner. The memo had read, GUEST FEARED SUBSTANCE A HEALTH HAZARD; MOVED TO SIMILAR ROOM AT REDUCED RATE TO APPEASE. The cleaning women were yelled at and the manager didn't believe them when they swore it wasn't there before, that they'd have seen it.

Nan turned off the light and took the stairs to the second floor balcony. She pressed herself against the wall between rooms 211 and 212 and listened hard over the increasing winds, mentally rehearsing what she would say if they caught her: *I forgot to give you a second keycard. Here you are. Have a nice evening.* A shadow passed back and forth across a narrow line of light spearing through the curtains and onto the walkway.

"Go . . . dinner?"

" . . . order in."

"But . . . to go out . . . got dressed up."

A pause.

"Okay," he said. "I'll just get dressed. Hey—did I leave my cigarettes in the car?"

His voice sounded loud. Close. Nan inched away from the door and ran through the breezeway to the stairs on the opposite side.

She watched the parking lot through the window and counted money while Diana, night-shift auditor, catalogued check-in receipts.

"Any problems?" Diana said.

Nan shook her head.

"What happened here?" Diana held up the Mackelroy receipt.

"Doesn't it say?" Nan was trying to hear the TV. They were saying something—broadcasting images of various banks of the Euphrates—but it was nothing. Nothing new. She stroked the lump the phone made in her pocket.

"Did you go look for yourself?"

"Yeah," Nan said. "Blood. Like it says."

"That's disgusting."

"M-hm."

She saw them, then, looking up at the sky on the way to their car. The girl had changed into a small dress, and Tanner wore a button-down. She wondered if he wore cologne and what it smelled like.

She wondered where they were going and didn't want him to leave.

"I wonder why I never get this many complaints when I'm working," Diana said. "You've had to move five people in two weeks."

Nan shoved the drawer into the register and took off her name tag. "It's busiest between two and ten," she said.

"Oh, hey." Diana held up a credit card. "This was on the floor when I came in. Mackelroy."

Nan said she would be happy to deliver it on her way out.

Light from the walkway dusted room 212 in orange. On the bed, an open suitcase and a stuffed green duffel bag. Between them, a plastic men's-store sack.

They hadn't mussed the covers.

That was usually the first thing people did.

Nan sniffed the air and smelled man. And hairspray. She found the hairspray and spritzed it, stuck her nose into the mist. Grape-y.

His folded ACU's made a neat stack on the chair. Nan traced the seam of a breast pocket with her thumb, slipped in the credit card, then picked up the top and pressed it to her face, but it was too much, toomuchtoomuch, so she put it down and went to the dresser and smoothed her fingers along the surface, grabbed a beaded necklace and touched loose change, earrings, a box of green tic-tacs.

Such privacy they'd created in just minutes with their clothing, their little things, their scents. The air was heavy with their presence and Nan thought of Christmas lights strung under snow, or of the soft melody made by a body moving under bathwater in a still room, and she was there, right in the middle of it, drowning in it, but not really, because even with her eyes closed and her fingers clutched around the girl's necklace and her breathing deep to take it all in and make it hers, it wouldn't take, and trying to be a part of it was like trying to throw a lasso around a ghost. It wasn't hers for the having, not for a long time, not until Marc came back, and he wouldn't be back. Not for a long time. She let go of the necklace and picked up the hairspray and sprayed it in her mouth because it was the only thing in the room she could ingest, but it didn't taste like grape, not at all. It tasted the way bug spray smelled, and it burned.

"Fuck." She spit on the floor and felt her tongue and lips swelling. "Fuck." She started for the bathroom to rinse out her mouth when she heard movement, talking, outside.

" . . . just so tired. I'm really sorry, babe."

Nan hurried to the space between wall and bed. There was just enough room for her to crawl underneath.

The carpet dug into her elbows and smelled like dust.

Their feet came in, a set of heels and a pair of black leather shoes. The heels stopped near a chair, crossed one over the other, and then slid off. The black leather shoes stopped at the end of the bed, and it bowed when he sat.

They were quiet. Nan imagined them smiling. Looking at one another without knowing what it meant that they could. So quiet, so quiet, and Nan had to swallow but was afraid they would hear. She opened her mouth and a pool of saliva dripped down.

The leather shoes shifted, toes pointing outward. "Sorry about dinner. You got all dressed up, and . . . " He trailed off.

The girl's toes curled. "Well, I *wanted* . . ." She sighed. "Anyway. We don't have to do everything tonight."

He moved on the bed. Turning toward the girl, Nan guessed. He said, "Everything?"

"You know. All these things that—just stuff I thought would be fun, you know, and—"

"Do you have a lot planned? Something every day?"

"No . . ." She sounded beaten. "Well, yes, actually, but don't you want—"

"Oh, yeah. Yeah."

Nan heard him take, and then release, a deep breath.

"Listen," he said. "Would you mind if we just kind of hung out and watched TV?"

"TV?"

"It's just . . . " He used the toe of one shoe to push off the other. "It's been eight months, you know, since I could do that."

Nan watched the girl's feet, which had become still.

"I—if you want to."

He took off his other shoe. "Cool."

The girl climbed on the bed. Nan heard her sniffing, and then the TV powering on.

The bed squeaked. "Sorry," said the girl.

"It's all right. Hey, you like this show?"

Nothing.

"Hey?"

"Hm?"

"I said, you like this show?"

"It's all right, I guess."

One television character said something to another and the other made a noise—Nan couldn't see what was done from underneath the bed—and she heard Tanner laugh loud with the laugh track.

"Tanner?" said the girl, so low Nan barely heard her. She wondered if she might have imagined it. But, there again: "Tanner?"

He laughed, said, "Ahhhh, shit."

Nan tried to stay under, tried to keep herself from clawing out and standing over them screaming, her mouth numb from wanting, wanting what they had if only they knew it but they didn't and she hated them.

Tanner scrambled toward the phone, Jennie toward the door, but soon, shamed for not doing not saying not being, they were back on the bed, fingers—her right hand, his left—pretzel-locked and white. They guarded their faces when Nan threw their shoes, Tanner rising just a little to say, as if to a private, "That's enough, now."

Nan slumped to the floor to check her phone for a signal. She moved it this way, that way, never getting more than two bars, and her lips felt sticky and thick when she said, "Can you turn on the news?"

Jennie found the channel and she and Tanner went to her. Each held one of her arms, stroked her shoulders, her back, her hair, until she calmed.

But there was no news.

Some minutes after midnight they helped her up and walked her to her car in the rain.

Katrina Denza

Snake Dreams

As soon as I pull into my father's driveway, a light goes on inside the condo. I don't have to wonder what he's doing up this time of the morning; he's always had a knack for knowing what I'm up to.

He's there, under the bare bulb outside his front door when I climb out of my car.

"What's happened, Eva?" The red stripes and lime background of his pajamas glow like a marquee under the light. Proof of his last girlfriend's lack of taste.

"I need a place to crash."

I slink past him, his peculiar smell of cooked onions and Old Spice a comfortable annoyance. I unzip my jacket and lay it on the hall table.

My father stands near the door, scratching his chest, his eyes not fully open. "You're okay then?"

"We'll talk in the morning, Dad."

"I don't have the sofa made up."

"I'm capable." I stretch up to give him a kiss and catch the side of his rough chin.

From the hall closet, I grab a couple of mismatched sheets and a blanket. I walk into the living room, suddenly drained, and yank the sofa flat into the bed position. It creaks and lands in place with a thud. My clothes reek of the club: spilled beer and smoke. I take them off and throw them into the corner of the room, nearly knocking over my father's lamp. I slip into the cold sheets and adjust my back so I'm not right on top of the metal bar that runs down the middle of the bed. Sometimes when I lie on it, I imagine this absurd, elongated version of myself draped around the pole in my mother's closet like a snake on a branch. As if I could go back in time and scare her away from her future.

The sum of what my mother left: one shell pink blouse with a rust stain near the bottom hanging on her closet's iron pole. I was eight when I ran into my parents' bedroom, so sure my father was mistaken. When I slid open my mother's side of the closet, the door catching for a moment in its groove, the emptiness of that rectangular space was the loudest thing in the room. And the shirt, still swinging slightly from the breeze of the door's

motion, invited me to tear it from its padded hanger, to dive into its
pinkness headfirst. What I should have done was mold it into a ball and
stuff it into my mouth. Instead, I stood there and yelled, hoping she'd hear
me.

In the morning, I wake to my father grinding coffee. He's singing along
with some country tune on the radio. I dress and try to push the bed back
into a sofa without him noticing, but somehow he hears the springs over the
whine of his music. He pokes his head into the living room.

"Ready for some eggs?" he asks.

The thought of it flips my stomach.

"I've gotta go."

"Not before you tell me what's going on," he says. His voice has
turned hard-edged. A warning. "Come have juice and toast."

My father's kitchen is a miniature replica of the one in our old
house. It's painted a similar yellow—a yolky color, the same little kitchen
table and chairs sit in the middle, the window over the sink has the curtain
with the ducks, and the fridge is covered with all the old magnets. This
kitchen is more efficient though, and safer, as it holds no memories.

I pull out a chair and sit. My father's hips jiggle as he scrambles the
eggs.

"What?" he says when he sees the look on my face.

Smiling, I tell him he's the weirdest person I know.

"So why do I have the honor of making breakfast for you once
again?" He scrapes the eggs out onto two plates and drops the hot pan into
the dish water. It sizzles before sinking.

"Myria locked me out."

He sets our food on the table and joins me. "What did you do?" he
says.

Of course he knows it's something I've done. Myria's pissed
because I slept with her boyfriend—not that I blame her, but her reaction is
a bit extreme considering the circumstances: Frank and I were both a little
drunk, I was having an emotional moment, and we have no plans to do it a
second time.

"It wasn't working out," I say. My eggs are runny but I slide a
forkful onto my toast anyway. "I might move in with Jim. He's been bugging
me about it."

My dad's face is almost a square. Sometimes, when I'm mad at him,
I call him Blockhead—never out loud. It's like the rest of his body,
substantial, not flabby. He wears his hair short against his head which makes
his reddened ears stand out against his tan skin. I know he's thinking about
telling me I can live with him; he's got that I-don't-want-to-appear-too-eager-
look.

"Don't even say it."

"Why not?" He shakes his head and peppers what's left of his eggs. "You could enroll in school again. Live here for free. It's ideal."

If I wanted a nun's life.

"No, thanks." I get up and walk over to rinse my plate. There's no view of the back yard through the window over the sink. In our old house I could see the willow tree, close to the house, and further back, three gnarled apple trees I used to climb. I used to sit under the willow with my mother until the heat of summer came and the needle-like legs of Japanese beetles made me cry. Before the bugs, she and I would sit in a circle of cool shaded grass and pluck it clean of buttercups and daffodils. Yellow was my favorite color then. Here, through the smaller window above my father's new sink, there's only a peek at a brown painted fence and a patch of dun-colored grass.

"I'm picking Jim up from the airport tomorrow," I say.

"You working tonight?"

I nod. He tells me I can stay another night. There's something he needs to talk to me about, he says. He glares down at his plate as he talks.

I kiss the top of his head and tell him I'll see him later.

The wind whips at my face as I slide into my car. My foot pumps the gas to keep it from stalling and I wait while it warms up. The sky is a wall of gray threatening to push down and smother all things beneath. It feels like snow. I wonder what it would be like to live in a warm climate. The week after my mother left, my father told me she went to live in Kenya. I was in fourth grade and not long after I heard the name, I got up the nerve to stay after school and ask my teacher how far away it was. He got this funny look on his face and nodded. He asked me to wait a minute and walked out the door and down the hall. He came back with a book on Africa. I took it home and never brought it back.

I read Kenya was another country on another continent. It had a desert, jungle and a snow-capped mountain. It also had lions, giraffes and snakes. Over a hundred and twenty different kinds of snakes. For years after, snakes slithered through my dark imagination. In my dreams, they hung from trees above my head, waiting for the chance to drop on me; or I'd watch, helpless, as a snake swallowed my mother whole, like the snakes I watched gorging on eggs three times the size of their heads on Mutual of Omaha's "Wild Kingdom." Or I'd have nightmares of my mother showing up in my room with snakes wrapped around, and springing from, her body.

I knock on my apartment door and this time Myria answers.

"You," Myria says, opening the door wider. "Come in."

It's weird how the place already feels as if it's rejected me even though all my stuff is still inside. I walk past Myria and grab a stool by the breakfast counter.

"We need to talk," I say.

"You're a bitch," Myria says. She walks over to the sink and slides two mugs off a rack that hangs over it. "Want caffeine?"

"Yeah, sure," I say, grateful. "You changed the locks."

Myria spoons instant coffee into the cups. "You fuck my boyfriend and expect to still live with me? Come off it, Eva. Besides, we need the room for Frank's office stuff. He's moving in, and there's no way you and he are going to be in the same room, alone, again."

Frank wears a dog collar and has a thing for rubber masks. He's always pulling one out of his jeans. Last month when the three of us went to Dairy Queen, the girl working the counter screamed when he yanked Brad Pitt's face down over his own. She later told us she was scared he was going to pull out a gun. The night Frank and I slept together, Myria had flown to Florida to see her mother. It started out all right—we sat on the sofa watching this movie, Rabbit Proof Fence. A part of me watched the movie like a normal person and another part of me identified with the girl who fights so hard to get back to her mother. Except I didn't fight; I didn't do a thing. And then I was bawling and Frank was rubbing my hair and telling me I was going to be fine and then his mouth was on mine and all I wanted was to stop crying and feel something else. When we were done, I wiped my stomach off with his shirt and threw it at him. "Asshole," I yelled. He picked up his shirt and stormed out of the room shaking his head.

Myria hands me a cup of black coffee. "We're out of milk," she says.

The coffee burns my throat—part of my penance.

"Even if you hadn't totally screwed up by messing with Frank, it wouldn't have worked out anyway," Myria says. She leans against the stove, her fingers wrapped around her own coffee. "You're a pain in the ass to live with. You constantly boss me around, leave these tight-ass notes everywhere that tell me to pick up this, wash that. You change the way the place looks all the time and you don't even ask me. First you paint the living room some fuck-wad orange, then it's lilac the next month."

"You said you liked the orange."

Myria rolls her eyes. "I used to like you, Eva."

There's no emotion in her voice as she says this, as if she's over what happened. I know she probably isn't, and she and Frank most likely won't last more than a few weeks.

"Fine. I'll stay at my dad's tonight and when Jim gets back from his trip, we'll come pick up my things."

Myria looks relieved. "I won't be able to give you your half of the deposit for a while."

"Keep it," I say. I set my cup on the counter and go in my room to pack a few things.

On my way to work, I call Jim. He's in London visiting his expatriate sister and her family whom I've never met.

"How's England?"

"I miss you," he says.

"I'm homeless," I tell him. Jim and I met at the club where I bartend. He used to come in every weekend and one Saturday, after last call, I invited him to stay and have a drink with me. He went to UVM; I started at Castleton state and never finished. I wanted to be an anthropologist, but I couldn't stand all the requirement classes I had to get through first. He got his degree in Social Services and works in a home for troubled teens.

"Seriously? You and Myria have a fight?"

"Something like that."

"You know what I'm going to tell you."

I do know. He's been asking me to move in almost since we met. Why pay rent for a place to hang my clothes, he asks, when I could hang them at his place for nothing. It's a nice sentiment, but it's never for nothing.

"Okay."

"What do you mean, okay?"

"I'll move in."

I move the phone away from my head when Jim yells, "Yes!"

"I'm staying with Dad, tonight. When I pick you up we'll talk about getting my things over to your place.

"I can't wait to see you," he says. "And other things," he adds. His soft laughter irritates me. There's always been something proprietary about Jim. My chest is beginning to feel tight and I'm not even there yet.

"I have to go. I'll be late."

At work, Mavis has already set up the bar. She gives me the evil eye as I walk by into the kitchen to punch in. She won't be mad for long—it's not as if I haven't covered for her before. It's a Tuesday night and the live music is mediocre, so the dance floor's empty except for the mentally-challenged kid that always stands and bounces next to the front speaker and Anita, our local transvestite. Most of the night, Mavis and I lean against the beer coolers and watch the band.

We offer last call at 11:00. Two guys near the bar talk about heading up the street to the corner pub for pool. I let it slip to Mavis during clean-up I might be looking for a place to live. I don't know why—I've already told Jim I'd move in with him. As it turns out, she tells me she knows this guy, a friend of her boyfriend, who wants a roommate. "He owns a house on Maple," she says.

"Jim would flip," I say.

"What's the big deal? It's not like you're signing up to sleep with the guy."

"He would," I insist.

Mavis shrugs.

My father is up when I get home around 11:30. He's wearing a different pair of pajamas—orange footballs on a background of electric blue. As far as I know he's never played football in his life.

I drop my bag on the kitchen table and put the kettle on for tea.

"You'll be up all night," my dad says, following me in.

"It's chamomile. Didn't you want to talk or something?" I walk back to the sink and wash my face with dish soap. Eyes closed, I hold my hand out for a towel and my father pulls one out from the drawer.

"Make one for me, too," he says, sitting down at the table. His sigh collapses into a soft whistle.

When they're ready, I grab our cups of tea and join him. He rubs his face in his hands as if he's trying to wake up.

"You're doing it again."

"What?"

"Blowing it. First it was college—"

"You hated that I wanted to be an anthropologist." He's an accountant, something practical and he never fails to remind me of this.

"People get an anthropology degree when they don't know what the hell they want. It's beside the point, since you didn't finish." He leans back in his chair, studies my face. "You're always getting kicked out. Why? For Christ's sake, tell me why you have such a hard time with people?"

"Have you noticed most people are stupid?"

"Antagonistic." He hits the table.

"That, too."

"I'm talking about you. You're deliberately antagonistic." He gets up from the table, his leg bumping the edge and sending tea spilling over the rim of my cup, and leaves the room. When he comes back in, he has an envelope in his hand. He drops it on the table in front of me.

"What's this?"

"Open it."

I rip the top off the envelope and slide out a pair of tickets. It's a roundtrip to Kenya. My hands start to tremble. "What are these?" I demand.

"I booked these months ago. I wasn't sure if we should take the trip or not."

"Hold on there. What trip?" I'm sweating under my shirt.

My father sits and takes a gulp of tea, his solid hand dwarfing the bone-china cup. "I've set it up with your mother. She's expecting it. Expecting you."

"You know where she is? Dad, what the fuck is going on?"

"Your mother didn't just leave," he says, his voice low and gentle, "I was the one who made her go."

"Back up. Rewind. What are you talking about?"

"She met this woman, an activist, through the church she'd started going to. They made plans for a tree farm somewhere in Kenya. After a while, she asked me if she could take you. I told her no."

"So we could have been with her."

"Not we. You."

"I'm still confused."

"Your mother and I were splitting by then. She and this woman . ."

"Yes?" Why can't he spit it out already?

"They had a relationship."

"Lovers?"

He nods his head. "But it's more complicated than that. The point is, she wanted to take you with them and it wasn't going to happen as long as I was alive. You were everything to me. Still are."

I look around the room. I am overcome with the urge to throw something, but there's nothing. I stare down my father.

"I don't believe this shit!" I pick up the tickets off the table and hurl them across the room. "You lied to me! For years you've been lying."

"Listen, I . . ."

"No! I've heard enough for one fucking night."

"Your mouth."

"Fuck off!" I yell on my way out of the room.

The next afternoon, I pick Jim up from the airport and we drive back to his place. I think about the tickets once, at the airport, when I watch a mother and daughter walk through security together, but I keep them from my mind for most of the day.

Jim's apartment is really a duplex, set in one of the newer developments on the west side of town. It's neat and attractive in a sterile kind of way. Kind of like Jim.

Inside, we chow down on a couple of grinders we picked up on the way home, leaning over the coffee table and dropping slivers of onion and lettuce onto the greasy sandwich papers. Later, in the bedroom, the both of us still wet from the shower, Jim pulls me on top of him.

"How am I going to get any sleep now that you're in my bed?"

"I'm always in your bed," I say, letting him gnaw at my neck, my ear.

"Aw, but this is different. I get to have you anytime I want."

His hands knead at my boobs, clutch my crotch. I'm not in the mood. I'm thinking about the tickets and my mother. Sex and my mother are already too closely linked. It's usually when I'm close to getting off that I see her closet. See its emptiness, the pink blouse. It used to only happen once in a while. Lately, it's as if I've conjured it out of habit. Jim thinks he's brought me to this state of ecstasy, a feeling I deal with by scrinching my eyes shut and holding my breath. He's wrong. It's the picture of my mother's closet slashing through whatever desire I'm feeling that does it. As if it's telling me: Don't even think about letting go.

"I'm tired," I say. He's disappointed, but he won't say so—he thinks he has to suffer me in silence.

"I'm glad you're here," he whispers. His hand rubs my back for a couple of minutes and then he's snoring.

I lie in bed wondering how I'll ever be able to live with Jim and breathe at the same time.

In the morning, I call the guy Mavis told me about and he gives me directions over the phone. Outside, it's freezing—there's a thin blanket of snow on my car, on the ground. The place I'm looking for is on the east side of town, on one of the nicer tree-lined streets that leads out to the country club. I pull into a driveway when I get to the group of birches he said marked the start of his property.

The house is a contemporary wood and glass structure. I climb out of the car and run up the gravel path and knock on the door. The guy opens it. He has an interesting, angular face; he's tall, though slightly hunched, with wild hair and pale, thick lips.

"Todd," he says, shaking my hand. "Come in."

He helps me off with my coat and hangs it on a wooden tree in the foyer. "This way," he says, and I follow him through a series of rooms and down a long hall. At the end is a large suite. "Here's the room for rent," he says. "It's private on this side of the house. We'll hardly see each other."

I like the room. It has high ceilings, large windows with a view of a meadow and the mountains beyond. There's a nice space for a sofa and chair by the stone fireplace and I see a bathroom off to the right.

"What's across the hall?" I ask heading toward another room.

"That's Harold's room. My snake. Sorry, it's a mess."

I feel a needle-like heat spread over my face and under my arms. "A snake? You have a snake?"

"Red-tailed Boa from Brazil. Know anything about boas?"

Once a year, I'd go to this science museum with my elementary class. It had all these hands-on exhibits: a bees' nest behind a clear glass panel so we could watch them; a solar system display all lit up; a giant bubble maker. It also had a couple of snake exhibits—a drawer full of shed snake skins and a family of boas. I wouldn't go near the snakes. One year, a teacher threatened to send me out to sit on the bus alone until I told her, sobbing, nose dripping snot, that a snake had killed my mother. She didn't leave my side for the rest of the afternoon and before we got back on the bus, she snuck me into the gift shop and offered to buy me a piece of quartz if I didn't tell the other kids.

Inside the small room, boxes are stacked against one wall. On the opposite side of the room there's a large aquarium. Next to that is a table heaped with stuff: paper towels, plastic bags, newspaper, tongs.

"Where is it?" I ask, peering into the aquarium.

Todd tucks his arm around my waist and guides me over to the end of the aquarium. "There." He points to the corner.

Harold's just lying there, not moving, but it isn't much of a stretch for me to imagine him slinking out of his aquarium and across the hall to my bed.

"You're not afraid of snakes, are you?"

I keep staring at Harold. Force myself to look until the prickly heat fades.

"No," I say. "Of course not."

I look at Todd, at the amusement in his eyes, then back at Harold, curled up, looking like nothing more than a fat, harmless shoelace. With a head.

When I turn back to Todd, I study his face. His eyes, gray, are underlined by dark crescents beneath darker lashes. The lashes almost touch the top of his cheeks. His hair hangs in mushroom-colored dreads and his clothes hang loose and rumpled. It's his messiness I find sexy. I want to bury myself in his gorgeous messiness.

I pull him onto the floor by the aquarium. Harold moves a bit as we pass by him. I shudder. Just once. There's a salty-mint taste to Todd's lips, his mouth. I open my own mouth wide to make room for his tongue. Moving down his body I lift his shirt and kiss the skin near the top of his pants. Unzip his jeans.

Todd's erection rises up through the open zipper. His hands, reaching for my shirt, get caught up in the fabric. I help by pulling it over my head and undoing my bra. I bend down and lick him, watch him bob to the direction of my tongue. Todd gets up and moves around to go down on me. His braids tickle both of my thighs. After, he rises up on his elbows and we fuck. We get each other off fast, without talk. So fast, there's no time to think of anything—no closet, no Harold, just a plain white sheet of nothing but physical touch.

When it's over, I lie back, stare up at Harold's glass home, and wait for my breathing to settle. The morning sun's coming through the window and bouncing off the aquarium.

"I'll think about the room," I tell Todd as I kiss his cheek, his chin, his eyes. I pull my shirt back on. Lie down again to button my jeans.

He looks stunned, bewildered. "Sure. Yeah."

At the door, he watches me walk to my car. "Call me."

I don't answer him.

In a café downtown, I sit by a large window with a latte and a blueberry bagel, though I haven't touched the bagel. There's a guy in a cherry-picker hanging Christmas wreaths on the light poles along one side of the street. The layer of snow that fell in the night has melted in the morning's rising temperatures—there's only a few patches left in the shelter of shaded areas. Inside the coffee shop, a kid whines she wants ice cream and her mother snaps at her it's too early for ice cream. I think, give the girl some ice cream. She could be gone tomorrow, or in the next hour, even. The future cannot be taken for granted.

I think about my mother asking my father for permission to take me with her, him standing there, an unmoving wall of granite, probably sure she'd give up her ridiculous fantasy. Change her mind. Change who she was. I'm angry at both of them. At him for lying. For thinking he had the right to decide things for all three of us. And I'm pissed at her for allowing him to bully her into retreat. For choosing that woman over me.

I try to picture my father and me flying on a plane over the Atlantic and getting off on a tarmac on another continent to find the woman who gave me life and left me. I imagine her waiting there for us to step off the plane, her long hair messed by hot, dry winds. Or I imagine riding in a jeep, dust kicked up behind us, to find her in some school house, teaching kids how to spell or multiply. Or outside, showing them on bent knees how to fill deep holes with the life of trees. She sees me, stands up, sways a little. I run to her and wrap my arms around her body, surrender into the circle of hers, in that heat, in the land of snakes. It's been fourteen years, but it feels like nothing and forever all at once.

Steven Gillis

The Society for the Protection of Animals

Uniss had a plan. The situation was dire. No one refuted this, though we knew at first only what Uniss told us.

In her cage, on the floor of our apartment, Uniss did her best to turn. She said it was important to feel as they did, to better understand. I questioned the necessity, wondered, "If we're supposed to be sympathetic, shouldn't we be motivated more by instinct?"

Uniss told me to, "Think about what you're saying. How can you understand what you haven't experienced?"

I could have argued the point, said many things were intuitive, like hunger and love and the want to survive, that understanding them was overkill, but I knew what Uniss would say. She had a way of moving inside her cage, naked and on all fours, up on her toes and fingers, her spine arched as she had learned to do, leaving room so when invited in I could scoot flat on my back and lay beneath her, staring directly at whatever she chose to offer.

The first time Uniss told me about the dogs, I was studying for an exam, trying to wrap my head around Heisenberg's Uncertainty Principle. Heisenberg's theory—known as the Copenhagen Interpretation — challenged objective reality, insisted the position and momentum of a particle could not be predicted simultaneously with any consistent degree of accuracy as observation itself construed reality. I watched Uniss walk across the room. She showed me the newspaper, squeezed my arm, waited for me to read what there was then said, "It's real. Look at the pictures."

Uniss sold health supplements at the Vitamin Barn, educated people on HGH and Oxidation Reaction for aging, Saw Palmetto, Pygeum, Ginseng, Rose Hips and d-Alpha Tocopherol with Beta. Twice a week she attended classes at the University, studied chemistry and microbiology, planned on opening a homeopathic clinic one day, offering alternative medicines and organic remedies. I usually parked on the opposite end of the mall, closer to Music Mart where I worked part-time, but the day Uniss and I met I wanted an Orange Julius and came in from the east side. The Vitamin Barn also sold on consignment black reclining chairs with built in massagers.

Uniss sat in one of the chairs with the motor turned high. She had short
black hair, thin arms pushed pale through the half sleeves of her grey and
red Vitamin Barn shirt. I stopped in front of the chair, watched the vibrating
waves shake her. She didn't seem to mind my staring. After a minute I gave
my own body a shiver, let go from my ankles through my knees up to my
hips and shoulders and head like a human wave rolling up and down again.
Uniss laughed and asked if I was epileptic. I told her no, that I was just a boy
studying quantum mechanics.

We lived in Marshall Creek, far enough from Idlebrooke and the dogs to
ignore their troubles if we chose. Uniss said we couldn't. She yanked
at my arm through the bars of her cage as if pulling the chain to a lamp.
"This is real," she waited for the light to come on. "We have to do
something." Idlebrooke's city council had apparently made a mess of things,
altering ordinances, raising the cost of dog licenses, vaccines and ownership
fees, doubling the tax on breeders while restricting areas where dogs could
be walked. The new policies aggravated pre-existing problems, resulted in
more dogs left as strays and runaways and otherwise abandoned. Rather than
rescind the new laws, the council decided to invest in a special bounty. Men
with pickup trucks, station wagons and minivans trolled the city wielding
ropes, dart guns, enormous fishing nets and cans of Alpo.

    We went the next night to the Wet Whistle with a group of friends
where Uniss showed everyone the article in the paper. She described the
dogs in various stages of abuse, cried and coaxed us into indignation. We all
agreed, the news was bad. Someone, we said, should do something. We sat
inside the Wet Whistle and drank through our second and third pitcher of
beer, feeling good about ourselves for taking the matter seriously, for
recognizing the cruelty and madness and being able to bang the tabletop and
rant quite loud.

Uniss began having bad dreams. A month before she had found a novel
by J.R. Pick called, *The Society for the Protection of Animals*. Pick's book
was semi-autobiographical, addressed his experiences in the Terezin
concentration camp near Prague in 1943. Reading about the camps, Uniss
cut her hair even shorter, refused to eat more than once a day for nearly two
weeks, sustained herself on vitamin B, soy and wheat germ. She took a pen
and wrote a series of numbers on the underside of her right forearm, read
more books; *In My Hands*, by Irene Gut Opdyke, *The Diary of Anne Frank*,
and Elie Wiesel's *Night*. Uniss' dreams caused her to kick and moan.
Sometimes I tried calming her by stroking her nipples or rubbing lower the
way she liked. I didn't know what else to do, had no real answer for the way
she said she saw herself while sleeping staring up as if from underwater.

    We bought the cage at PetCo, a collapsible kennel, the largest they
had. Uniss wanted to see what living that way felt like. She had to duck and

fold herself to get inside. I fell asleep on the bed and woke mid-morning to find her in the cage, hunched down and reading a copy of Edmond Jabes *The Book Of Questions: Yael, Elya, Aely.* I joked with her, "You know, if its the experience you're after, dogs can't actually read." Uniss took this more seriously than I intended, slid the book out through the bars, barked twice and shook her head.

My sister, Shari, had a house near the University where she worked as a dietician. Shari was married to J.J. Leeme, a junior account manager at Spotlease payroll services. In 2002, J.J. had joined the National Reserves. Three months ago, he was called up and sent to Iraq. J.J. and Shari had a baby boy named Bill, but I called him Bubba for no reason other than I liked the sound. Two days after Uniss and I bought the cage, Shari phoned and told me she had cancer. "Carcinoma in situ," breast cancer that had yet to spread outside the duct or lobule. We contacted the army but they wouldn't let J.J. come home, said the paperwork would take at least a month and everyone should just wait and see how things panned out.

The doctors did the biopsy and started Shari on chemo. I took a week off from the Music Mart. My head was a mess. I struggled with my classes. I loved my sister and told Uniss, "I don't want her to die." In the shower, I checked Uniss' breasts with my fingertips, examined rather than caressed. Uniss indulged me. For Shari, she pulled out all her books, researched remedies, educated us on what ACT—Adriamycin, Cytoxan and Taxol— did to the body's white blood cell count, how chemo messed with the neutrophil which fought infections, creating neutropenia. She put Shari on a high iron diet, had her eat lots of green vegetables, told her to avoid red meat, salt and sugar and dairy, gave her natural remedies to work with the steroids and counter the poisons: Ipecacuanha and Phosphorus 30 for vomiting, Sepia for anaemia, Selicea to help boost her immune system.

At night, I lay with Uniss wherever she wanted. I couldn't sleep now without her near. When I thanked her again for Shari, she smiled. I remained outside the cage as Uniss inside slid her fingers down my cheeks before pulling her arms back, and stretching beside me with the bars between us, asked "Do you think the dogs they've caught are scared?"

The novelty of the cage turned problematic the second time Uniss and I tried having sex. Doggie-style, I banged my head against the top of the bars, had to hunch down until too much of my weight was resting on Uniss and I could barely thrust. She rolled her head around as if to snap, then laughed and collapsed and told me to, "Get out." A week after Shari started chemo, Uniss read that Idlebrooke was selling captured dogs for medical research. She came to find me at work and said she had a plan.

We drove the forty miles up Route 23 just before midnight. Along the way we listened to the news on the radio. With J.J. overseas, I paid more attention to the war. Dozen of people had died earlier that day in four separate explosions in Baghdad. Last night American soldiers raided the Ministry of Health, smashing doors and walls, confiscating money targeted for security workers. "Its endless," Dr. Ali al-Shimari, the Health Minister complained as an American spokesman said the soldiers were acting on a tip to stop the kidnapping of Prime Minister Nuri Kamal al-Maliki and his family. "We are only here to do the right thing." Uniss bought a huge pair of wire cutters and a large hammer with a flat barrel head. Dogs not yet sold to labs were held in cages stacked and spread out in a fenced area near the old armory.

We parked and walked across the street. The air smelled of gas and beer, changed to something more feral as we came nearer the fence. I looked for a guard, wondered about cameras and alarms as we went around back, away from the street and abutting a weed dry field. The dogs stirred but didn't bark as we cut through the wires. Even as we clipped the locks and hammered at some to break the bolts, they seemed to know and waited.

The first report came on the 5:00 a.m. news. Uniss and I fell asleep together in bed, woke and listened to the broadcast. "Over 500 dogs," the reporter claimed. "503," Uniss said. I didn't realize she'd counted. Uniss bit my shoulder. Setting the dogs free had made her happy. She slipped from bed and danced. I stared at her, saw the way her t-shirt rolled over the curve of her breasts, thought of what Wheeler said about the essence of reality and how, "No phenomenon is a real phenomenon until it's an observed phenomenon." I held out my arms, kicked off the sheet and asked her to, "Come back to bed and free this dog, baby."

At noon I left for Music Mart, feeling high and pleased and only vaguely worried about being arrested. Twice at work I joked by playing the Baha Men's "Who Let the Dogs Out" over the sound system. I had class that night and got home sometime after 10:00 p.m. to find Uniss sitting in front of our TV, the remote in her hand as she flicked back and forth between the local news channels. Dogs were shown in the streets, running between houses and buildings, on the lawns and through alleys in Idlebrooke. Six hounds were said to have been hit by cars while the hospital reported a record number of dog bites over the last twelve hours. Uniss stared at the television while I came and sat beside her, watching labrador and German shepherds, poodles and terriers and mutts of every conceivable combination dashing across the screen. I waited as Uniss reviewed what we failed to predict and considered again our options.

Niels Bohr and Werner Heisenberg, when first explaining quantum mechanics, viewed causation as a theory-specific concept varied in each new physical circumstance. Causation was broken into two components: causal connection and causal priority, with the space between described by Thomas Hausman as, "the undefined intuitive notion of a nomological linkage." All of this was rudimentary, before the real work

began, and the point where I tended to get lost. At its root, I understood
how no two interactions were identical, that observation altered and created
the universe individually for its observer as Wheeler said, and yet, outside of
ourselves and our own observations, shit still happened. But for our letting
the dogs out, none of the rest would have taken place, and what did it matter
then if we failed to witness it first hand?

Driving to Idlebrooke again, Uniss brought a leash and bait, found
the first dog just after we left Route 23. A brown-grey mongrel mix,
malamute and possibly brittany, shaggy from his withers down, his flews and
muzzle dark. I pulled up to the curb and Uniss got out of the car, sat on the
dew moist lawn with bacon strips and hands held out. The dog ran past,
came back, slowed and stared at us. From memory maybe or just hunger, he
moved toward Uniss, close enough to where she could pet and pull him in.

We rescued three dogs that night. Our apartment was small with
wood floors which created a click-click-click as the hounds moved about.
Pets were prohibited so we covered our front room and the space around
the cage with towels and sweaters. Saving three dogs seemed a finger in the
dike, but there was Uniss, happy again, sitting among the mutts, a pot of
water between her outstretched legs while the hounds together came and
drank.

I rested my back against the cage, across from Uniss on the floor.
We remained this way for some time. I had the early shift the next morning
at Music Mart and eventually crawled off to sleep. Uniss said she wanted to
stay with the dogs and get them settled. She promised to find them a place
to live tomorrow and agreed to arrange her work schedule to make sure this
happened. I woke to find her in the cage with the malamute mutt, the other
two dogs asleep nearby. The food we bought the night before was poured
into my favorite cereal bowl. At some point while I slept Uniss had taken the
hounds into the bathroom and washed them. When I tried to shower I
found the drain thick with matted hair and my one remaining towel soaked
and covered with foul dog scum. The dogs watched me move about the
apartment, remained observant until I left.

The mall was a ten minute drive. I bought a paper at lunch and read
another story about the dogs. To my surprise, Idlebrooke had extended
its bounty, the only revision to the original deal was that the hounds now
caught had to be brought in dead. I called Uniss but she didn't pick up. After
work I drove out to my sister's house. The chemo had killed off Shari's hair.
She wore a scarf and pretended for Bubba's sake to be playing a part in a
Mother Goose fable. The homeopathic remedies Uniss provided offered
some relief, but the poison was cumulative. Shari had sores in her mouth
and between her toes. I dangled Bubba above her, brought him close where
she could kiss him. "At least the cancer will be gone," I wanted to hint of

promise. Shari smiled as if she'd completely forgotten, said "The treatment was a success doctor, but the patient died."

We watched TV together, some late afternoon sitcom and a bit of the news. Shari looked for hints of J.J. in the coverage. The local news ran even more stories about the dogs, stock footage showing the hounds dashing about a few days earlier. Many of the freed dogs had made their way to Marshall Creek where rumors of a rabies outbreak gave a false excuse to those eager to collect on the bounty. I called Uniss again but still there was no answer.

At class that night we reviewed the Copenhagen Interpretation, assessed observation, causal connection and phenomena. We discussed Gell-Mann and Feynman. As an aside, Prof. Finkel mentioned the Poincare Conjecture, which dealt with the nature of space. I was lost when the problem was presented. "If any loop in a certain kind of three-dimensional space can be shrunk to a point without ripping either the loop or the space, must the space then be equivalent to a sphere?" My head ached to even think where to start, and seeing my puzzled look, Finkel quoted Poincare with a smile. "Thought is only a flash in the middle of a long night, but the flash that means everything."

The quote helped me relax. I pictured three-dimensional spheres and tubes, soap films and dogs, saddles and the flare of a trumpet spread out for 12,500 miles. Driving back to the apartment after class, I thought more about causality and the theories of Hausman, Barrett, Einstein and Bohr. I parked the car and hurried up the stairs, opened the door and called to Uniss. The three dogs from yesterday were huddled in the far corner while several new hounds now filled the room. An akita mix came to sniff me, followed by a doberman and Finnish spitz. A retriever stood on our couch while the rest of the mutts moved closer.

Uniss was in the cage, sitting with her back against the right side. "Here, quick," she called to me just as a large mastiff mix moved toward me. I stared at the cage, then at the doberman raising the sides of his muzzle, showing me teeth. The mastiff pushed through the other hounds. I pictured Uniss, hearing the news about the latest bounty, driving around in search of strays, loading up her car more than once, sneaking the dogs into our apartment and for what? I turned my hips, rolled my fingers, the dogs now in a collective snarl. Only the three mutts from the night before hung back, each appearing to have been attacked earlier, the malamute I noticed with a bloodied haunch, the others with torn crests and withers and ears. The mastiff mix was black and broad and as he bit my thigh the strike was less savage than calculated. I screamed then dove past the other hounds.

Uniss opened the latch to the cage and pulled me in. We had to squirm and roll and hunch down to fit. I looked at the tear in my pants, examined the bite, which was already blue beneath the blood. "What the fuck?"

I observed the dogs and saw them circle, thought of Einstein who disagreed with Heisenberg, was convinced in a causal, objective reality, argued that a real world existed independent from any act of perception. Accumulated knowledge should have told us what would happen, given us objective reality, confirming a constancy in causality which Heisenberg and Bohr otherwise denied. I modified the Uncertainty Principle to fit our situation, how Heisenberg said it was impossible to correctly gauge the position and momentum of any one particle at the same time. If our position was to help the dogs, the momentum of our act had failed to create a simultaneously accurate value as our inspiration sailed too far out ahead of where we needed to land. All the unintended phenomena was organic, like space and time expanding and collapsing, everything passing through stages, the nomological linkage, until everything that could be became apparent.

Theresa Boyar

Waxing Razal

Sometimes, sheet lightning over the orange groves, the sky slate blue and heavy with electricity. Sometimes there's a light rain trickling down through the leaves. One night my sister Gracie wears jeans. The next night, the ropes are wound tight around her favorite pajamas, the ones with white rabbits and a satin trim patterned with lettuce heads and carrots. It's the same dream, the only dream I've had for more than sixteen years. Each time, there are minor variations.

I dream I'm twelve years old again, or else I'm my current age, the hard spine of an orange tree pressed up against the clinical coat I wear to work, the ropes cinching my wrists.

Without exception, Gracie is always fourteen.

Tonight, I dream her hair is gathered in a ponytail. Stray blond ends cling to her face, which has lost its summertime complexion, its haunting flawlessness, and is instead a confusion of sweat, dirt, and tears.

Lucy, my sister's best friend, is there the way she always is—an unseen being amid the neat rows of trees. There's more of an awareness of Lucy than actual physical presence. I know that somewhere in the groves, she too is bound tightly to a tree, only her head is hanging forward, her body is motionless, her taunting voice inexorably silenced.

Despite the slight alterations my mind makes in the weather and Gracie's clothing, the action always progresses the same way. Geoffrey Beldon picks up his baseball bat, and I scream from an opposite tree while my sister's face goes black with blood.

I never awaken until Geoffrey finishes with my sister and turns toward me. He raises the glistening bat in the air, and at the first sign of downward motion my eyes are shocked open, my lungs aching so hard they feel as if they'll crack apart.

I've accepted that this dream will never go away, that it has grown through my life the way tree roots spread beneath the ground. Unseen. Expanding. Constricting.

I awake with my usual post-dream headache and tap two orange capsules into my palm from the bottle I keep on my nightstand. I swallow them dry while shuffling into the bathroom, the blood-spattered image of Geoffrey Beldon traveling with me, still strong and clear.

My dreams increase in frequency like this each year around the anniversary of the murders. The media uproots the story and suddenly, Gracie and Lucy smile at me from my television set. Suddenly, I can smudge my thumb across the local newspaper and transfer the ink of my sister's eyes to my skin. Their story is dredged up as a warning to parents, a gruesome reminder that despite South Florida's lustrous exterior of scenic beaches and beautiful people, the place is not without its share of monsters.

The story has evolved over time, so that now footage of Geoffrey Beldon is spliced between interviews with internet experts, cautioning parents that today's predators are lurking not just in orange groves, but in chat rooms as well. Occasionally, there will be an interview with my mother, and I'm always surprised by a new hairstyle, the deepening of the lines across her forehead, the thickening of the skin on her neck.

My father is never mentioned. He's a distraction from the core drama, a bleak side note whose story is separate from Gracie's. Nobody wants to see the connection, the way Gracie's murder slowly consumed more and more of him through the years, until there was nothing left.

In the news coverage, the parting shot is always the same: a close-up of Lucy and Gracie taken at Disney World, though it's impossible to tell the photo was taken at Disney because the background has been cropped out. In the original photo, the gray and blue spires of Cinderella Castle rose bright and enormous behind them, and if you looked closely at the crowd, you'd see a six-foot chipmunk signing an autograph book for a young girl who is me.

In the shower I work hard to replace Geoffrey Beldon's face with a mental rundown of my clients for the day. Three massages in a row. Mrs. Krellan at nine, the first appointment, and also the worst. She's seventy years old and her skin is so loose and dry on her frame that when I touch her, I'm afraid she'll peel apart in my hands.

After her is Mr. Stein, a businessman bent on reclaiming a stress-free mentality. He's followed by Janna, a twenty-year-old yoga instructor who brings in spotty produce from her organic garden as a treat for the staff. I have a block of free time in the early afternoon, when I can expect to take a few walk-ins, or, if business is slow, sweep the rooms and tidy the reception area. My last hours at the salon will be spent in the waxing room.

I try to schedule my waxing appointments for late afternoon, so I can get the massages out of the way first. I prefer waxing, not because I'm a closet sadist, but because massages always leave me feeling as if something has been taken from me. I knead my fingers into my clients and it's my warmth, the friction I create, that relaxes their muscles, that renders the sighs that escape their lips so often. I feel as if my clients borrow something from me during massages. Something is taken with no hope of it ever being returned.

Waxing is different on so many levels. There's the idea of pain versus pleasure, to be sure, but there's something else as well. For me, waxing feels more professional, less intimate. It's easier to separate myself from the people on my table. Plus, although I haven't been to church since I was twelve, I've attended enough Sunday school classes to know to feel guilty when a sixty-year-old man rises after a half-hour massage and hunches over his erection, trying to cover it up with the stiff white towels the salon provides.

I head into work and there's a message from Mr. Stein that he needs to cancel his appointment due to an unexpected meeting. It works out well because Janna shows up early. She settles a paper sack of oranges on the front desk, and tells me she picked them herself from the tree behind her house. She holds the bag open for me and I glimpse a small mound of fruit, mottled in colors of yellow and pale green and masked with a network of brown scars.

I haven't eaten an orange in years. The thought of it alone is enough to set my stomach on edge, but I tell Janna they look great and thank her for bringing them in.

I'm stretched out on my bed, arms folded across my stomach, while Lucy and Gracie rummage through Gracie's underwear drawer.

"I know they were here," Gracie says, "I put them here myself."

The two of them pull the drawer out of the bureau and turn it upside down. Their hands swim through a pile of pastel underwear and floral-print bras. Lucy stands up and reaches into the empty cavity in the bureau where the drawer has been removed. I know I should leave the room, but I'm paralyzed by a need to see how this plays out. Then, almost at the same time, Lucy and Gracie put their hands on their hips and swivel in my direction.

"You took them," Gracie points at me.

"Took what?" I'm a terrible liar and have to concentrate all my energy on avoiding eye contact with the closet, where the letters I stole from Gracie's drawer are hidden inside the pocket of my plum corduroy skirt.

Lucy rolls her eyes and walks over to the side of my bed, breathing heavily and glaring. She stands above me and I can smell her sweat mixed with the baby powder she and my sister sprinkle into their bras.

"Where are they?" she yells.

I start to sit up, but Lucy pushes me back down.

"I asked you a question."

I tell her I don't know what she's talking about but she grabs a fistful of my hair and threatens to pull it out. I look at Gracie, who is standing at the foot of my bed.

"Come on, Lucy," she says. "Maybe I left them in my locker."

Lucy releases my hair and I sink back into my pillow. I hear our bedroom door close, followed a few seconds later by the softer thud of the front door. I walk into the living room and peek outside to make sure they have left, and when I see their bikes round the corner at the end of our street, I head for my bedroom closet.

What I notice first about the letters is the penmanship. The handwriting is looped and elegant, reminding me a little of my mother's but with less of a rush to it. There are five letters. They all begin with "My Dear Lucy" or "Dearest Lucy." Before I read them, I flip to the end and read the same closing on all five letters: "Forever yours, Geoffrey."

I imagine Geoffrey to be one of the older boys in the high school, and in my mind he becomes sandy-haired and lanky, with searing eyes and gentle hands. I read paragraph after paragraph, all proclaiming Geoffrey's undying love for Lucy. He tells her he wants to run away, just the two of them, and live on an island somewhere. He says he wants to breathe her in, to taste her, to swallow her.

I sit on the closet floor reading, and all I can think is that I would give anything to be Lucy, to have a boy fall this madly in love with me. In the last letter of the series, Geoffrey writes that he has watched Lucy in gym class that day. He talks about the smoothness of her legs, the way her hair gleamed. He tells her he loves her and says again that he wants to run away with her, and I feel a tug from somewhere behind my navel.

I hold onto the letters for two weeks, reading them over and over when I'm alone, until I have most of them committed to memory. When I finally decide to burn them to avoid being caught, I stand over the bathroom sink crying, letting the pages burn down to my fingers before dropping them into the basin.

Janna leaves, flexing her neck back and forth as she exits, and I take my first coffee break. On the way to the employee lounge, I pass Marjun, the salon owner, and she tells me that Razal called and will be in to see me within a half hour.

"Don't get too cozy back there," she says.

Razal is the only massage client I look forward to seeing. He's a large, stout man in his mid-sixties and he has a habit of talking throughout the massage. In his thick Middle Eastern accent, he tells me stories about the people in his apartment complex. He has no children of his own, but the younger kids in his neighborhood call him Poppa and come to him when they've fallen off their bicycles or when their parents are arguing indoors. When he talks about these children, I find it hard to stop my mouth from watering at the mention of the butterscotch disks and milky caramels he doles out freely to them.

Lately, Razal has been talking a lot about Mrs. Wickham, the widow who lives on the first floor, directly beneath his apartment. He hears her late at night, flicking the television on and off, opening and shutting a window. He claims he can hear her sighing.

"An undecided soul," he says of her, "So alone, so afraid."

From what he's told me, I'm fairly certain that the chances of Mrs. Wickham returning his affections are slim to none, though I would never say this to Razal. I say, in fact, very little to him. When he first began coming in, I worried that my silence would discourage him from talking. But that was two years ago, and he continues to fill me in on the latest details of his life while I continue to quietly absorb them.

Razal has a way of making even the most mundane activities sound extraordinary. Last month, he told me about finding a spider in his bathroom. Rather than kill it, he lifted it from the floor with a sheet of newspaper and deposited it in a houseplant on his coffee table. He told me that this plant would make the spider very happy, because he knew there were tiny gnats living in its soil. A couple of days later, Razal took a nap on his couch, his left hand stretched out on the coffee table. When he awoke, there was a red swelling near the base of his thumb and the spider was making its way along his inner wrist.

"And what," Razal asked, "do you think of that?"

He doesn't seem to mind that I don't answer his questions. He chuckles or sighs and goes right into his next story. By the time he leaves my massage table, I feel as if there's a balance between us, like I've received from him as much as I've given.

During his most recent appointment, he told me about Mrs. Wickham's grocery sack ripping as she passed through the courtyard. He had been sitting in a shady spot, playing rummy with three other men from the building. When he saw her vegetables spill, he jumped up to help, and after capturing her rolling tomatoes, he thought he was doing her a favor by telling her she had made a poor choice.

"They were too soft," he said, "and it wasn't from the fall. I felt them. I smelled them. I could tell they were all wrong inside. Mealy. Gritty. Who wants to eat tomatoes like that?"

Mrs. Wickham wasn't very happy to receive his advice, he said. She plucked the tomatoes from his hand and marched away.

"Like a soldier," he laughed, "like an angry soldier."

What I like most about Razal is the way it feels as if I'm holding an earthquake in my hands whenever he laughs, which is often.

The employee lounge is empty. I pour myself a cup of coffee. Someone has emptied Janna's oranges into a large bowl and stuck a card inside that says, "Delicious! Have one." I lift the metal folding chair and twist it away so I don't have to look at them.

It's dusk and Gracie is stuffing pajamas and a change of clothing into her backpack. Lucy stares at herself in the mirror, coiling a blond curl around her finger and releasing it, watching it spring back into place. She bends in close and detaches a tiny clump of mascara from an eyelash, blinking several times before turning to check Gracie's progress.

"Hurry up," she says, "he'll be waiting."

They can say this in front of me because I already know the truth. I was standing at the bedroom window while Lucy and Gracie, wearing bikinis and sprawled on lawn chairs in our backyard, discussed their plans. I also know they lied. Gracie told our parents she will spend the night at Lucy's house, and Lucy told hers she'll stay at Gracie's. Instead, they are meeting Geoffrey in the orange groves near the high school.

Actually, Lucy is the one meeting Geoffrey. Gracie is a tag-along, a lookout. She will patrol the orange groves and clap three times if she sees anyone.

When I heard Geoffrey's name mentioned by the window, I put my hand on Gracie's desk and leaned in closer. A stack of her papers slid off the edge, some landing on the chair with a thud, others spilling noisily to the floor. In less than a minute the girls were in the bedroom, warning me against telling anyone what I had just heard. I promised I would keep quiet.

Tonight, Lucy wears jeans, a red T-shirt, and sandals. She has painted her fingernails and toenails to match her shirt, and her lips gleam with a scarlet sheen. Gracie zips up her backpack and narrows her eyes at me. "Remember," she says, "not a word."

As they exit the room, I see a small bit of fabric hanging out of Gracie's backpack and recognize her rabbit pajamas.

The next day, a Saturday, my mother pushes gently on my shoulder. It's a little after noon and I haven't gotten out of bed yet, having spent most of the night awake, imagining what Lucy and Geoffrey have been doing in the orange groves.

My mother sits on the edge of my bed and tightens her robe around herself. On weekends, she and my father make something of a game of lounging in their robes for as long as possible.

She asks if I'm awake and I rub my eyes and mumble, "What?"

"I need to ask you something," she says. "I just spoke with Lucy's mother and she says the girls didn't sleep there last night. Do you know where they are?"

I pull my pillow over my head to avoid eye contact.

"No," I say.

My mother pulls the pillow away and stares directly at me.

"This is important. Gracie could be hurt or in trouble. Can you think of where they might be?"

"I said 'no'," I tell her, rolling over.

I feel my bed shift as it releases my mother's weight.

By two o'clock, my mother has called everyone in Gracie's phone book and Lucy's mother has done the same. Nobody has heard from either of the girls.

When the police come to get a description and borrow photographs, my mother sits on our sofa with her arms wrapped around herself, still in her bathrobe, rocking back and forth. My father provides all of the information. His voice is calm and even, intent on getting things right. But I can see his jaw clenching and unclenching, his eyes settling into a daze while he pauses and waits for the officer to transcribe his words.

I'm remembering the letter Geoffrey wrote to Lucy, telling her he wanted to run away with her. Clearly, this is what has happened. Gracie has gone with them for a few days, accompanying her best friend long enough for Lucy to feel comfortable with her decision. She will be back in a couple of days. There is no need to mention their secret meeting, the orange groves. They are not there.

The police leave and my mother moves her hands in front of her face, a wet tissue caged within her folded fingers. She is unable to still her body. When I place my hand on her shoulder, she stops abruptly and pulls me close.

Much later, I will recognize this as the first time I no longer want to be held by my mother. It is more than a sense of repulsion at her wet face and runny nose. It is the way she holds me from that day onward, not as if she is happy to have me, not as if she is hugging a daughter she loves, but she clings to me, needy and determined. If she squeezes hard enough, she can go through me to reach that other daughter, the one who has gone away.

When Gracie comes into my room that night, I sit up and start to ask questions. Where's Lucy? Did she run off with Geoffrey? What happened? What kind of punishment did she get?

But Gracie is silent. She stands near the door and opens her hand. An orange rests in her palm, and she tips her wrist up so that the orange falls and spins across our floor. Just before it rolls under my bed, I notice it is streaked with red.

I bend over the edge of my bed and look underneath but nothing is there. When I sit back up, Gracie is gone.

This is how I come to tell my parents, at two a.m., about the secret rendezvous with Geoffrey in the orange groves. I am crying when I tell them, terrified of what has happened in my bedroom. I do not tell them about Gracie standing by the door. I say nothing about the orange rolling under my bed. My parents believe I'm crying out of guilt from not having spoken up sooner.

My father calls the police and gives them the new information. They promise to head over to the orange groves, and check things out right away. The three of us go to the kitchen and sit around the table while we wait. My father makes tea, but I am the only one who drinks it. Tiny sips of clean hot liquid, oversweetened by my distracted father. My mother clutches her cup without drinking.

I hear Razal's voice from the employee lounge and brush off my lap, though I have eaten nothing that would leave crumbs. I rinse my cup, flip my chair back toward Janna's oranges, and head into the reception area. Razal smiles broadly when he sees me, and I can't help but smile back.

"There she is," he says. He holds his arms out as if he might hug me and I let myself imagine what that hug would feel like. Soft, warm, like falling into pudding.

Razal claps his hands together and rubs them. "Okay," he says, "I've got something different in mind today." I raise my eyebrows and he laughs and says, "Today, I find out if you are as skilled at waxing as you are at massage."

He says the word waxing as if it were two words: whack, sing.

"Waxing?" I ask, "You want me to wax you?"

He laughs again, nodding. I have massaged Razal so many times that I am familiar not only with his sand-colored skin, but with the rampant peppery curls of hair I rub down each session. I can't imagine his back swept clean.

He promises to explain everything and starts to head down the hall to the massage room. I tell him we use a different room for waxing. "Of course, of course," he says, and follows me down the opposite hallway.

In the room, Razal removes his shirt and reveals his large, fleshy middle. He reaches with one arm over his shoulder and points to his back.

"I want it all gone," he says, "back here. All of it. Pfffft."

I make it a rule never to question my clients' decisions, especially when it's clear that their minds are made up. Razal's is an unusual request, but if Mr. Stein had come in asking for the same thing, I would have distanced my mind from the task and performed without question.

Distance. Something at which I excel. Something for which I'm known.

For the past five years, during my work reviews with Marjun, the only criticism she's had is that I haven't made any real connection with the other employees. Distant is the word she uses each time.

I start to stir the wax, but stop and turn to face Razal. I'm only mildly surprised to find that my hands are shaking when I ask, "Why? Why do you want to do this?"

There's a flutter in my stomach and I feel as if I've just stepped off an elevator, the slick linoleum lurching beneath me. New ground.

Razal simply raises his shoulders and lets them fall again and tells me that he is in love.

"That Mrs. Wickham," he sighs, and shakes his head.

I lean against the counter while Razal tells me about an article he has read. They polled three hundred women and found that eighty-two percent of them preferred men with smooth bodies as opposed to hairy ones.

"It is the new masculine," he says.

I want to warn him that a smooth back will not make Mrs. Wickham love him. I want to tell him how doubtful it is that any of those three hundred women were elderly widows. But I look at my hands, still trembling, and instead I say, "It's going to hurt, you know. A lot."

He grins and waves his hand, dismissing my concern. "I trust you," he says, flipping over and resting his chin on folded arms. "Completely."

My mother breaks quickly, loudly. She screams when the policemen come to our door at five-thirty that morning and deliver the news that the bodies have been found. She shocks everyone by punching the taller man, Officer Davies, squarely in the face, hard enough to bring blood to the corner of his mouth. He doesn't get angry, but wipes the blood away with the back of his hand, and gently turns my mother around, pointing her back toward us, directing her anger inward.

While Officer Davies and my father settle on a time for us to meet at the station later that day, my mother begins with our teacups, sweeping them off the table in a wide arc of her forearm. The tea splashes over the refrigerator and makes a dripping amber mess of our kitchen.

My father rushes the men out the door, and once they're gone, my mother turns to the dining room and her Blue Willow display in the china cabinet. She wrecks everything inside, hurling it piece by piece across the room. My father and I sit together on the sofa, watching, terrified and amazed. I want to stop her, but my father holds me in place.

"Let her do this," he whispers in my ear, his voice cracking slightly.

So we sit together while my mother creates a magnificent mound of porcelain, a thin white dust settling over the tables and chairs, her hair chalking over. It seems she has aged twenty years.

At the police station later, I feel as if everyone is watching me. I walk through the maze of desks with my father, following Officer Davies. My mother is lost in a chemically induced sleep back home, neighbors around to keep an eye on her.

Officer Davies takes us to a small room, with a table and a few chairs. He brings out coffee for my father, a can of soda and a raspberry-cream cheese pastry for me, but the cream cheese has a parched look, cracked in places from sitting too long in this airless room.

The details of what happened in the orange groves have, for the most part, been kept from me, though I have heard the word *bludgeon*, a soft sounding word, which stung like a wasp in my throat when I looked up its meaning in the dictionary.

Officer Davies rubs the small scab that has formed on the side of his mouth and directs his attention to me. "What can you tell us about Geoffrey?"

In my head, an assemblage of characteristics I've imagined for so long gathers force. I picture the tall, soft-spoken boy whose features I have supplemented over the weeks so that by now they include bookish eyeglasses, a smile that whisks up higher on one end, and eyes the color of seagrass. The reality is that I know almost nothing about Geoffrey. I remember his penmanship, the contents of his letters.

"I think he was older than Gracie and Lucy," I say, "I think he was in Lucy's gym class."

"You've never met him?" Officer Davies narrows his eyes when he asks this, and when I shake my head in response, it feels like a lie.

On Monday the police inform us that Gracie's high school has three Geoffreys enrolled, and all of them have been cleared. They tell us they are looking into a school janitor with the same name who did not show up for work that morning. His record shows an assault charge against a former girlfriend. Officer Davies tells my father he is bringing over a photograph and would be grateful if I took a look at it.

He shows up within fifteen minutes and my father walks him into our living room. I hear my mother whimpering in her bedroom, even though the door is shut. My father asks if I'll be okay while he goes and checks on her. I nod.

Officer Davies does not trust me, I can tell. I wasn't forthcoming about the orange groves and now, apparently, I have provided false information about Geoffrey's identity. He opens a file and passes me a photo of a man with a small gash of a mouth and tight, angry eyes. He looks to be in his thirties.

"Look familiar?" Officer Davies asks.

I look at the narrow jaw, the hair that hangs like icicles around his forehead. I shake my head.

"No," I tell him truthfully, "Not at all."

Officer Davies eyes me closely. I feel my stomach twisting at the thought that the man in the photograph is Geoffrey, and I have to ask, I have to be sure.

"Is that him?" I ask, "Is that Geoffrey?"

There's a moan from my mother's bedroom that starts low and continues to rise in pitch until it evolves into a scream. I look at the floor. Officer Davies puts the photo back inside the file. He says nothing.

The following Sunday, the paper runs a special tribute to Gracie and Lucy, featuring an enlarged photograph of them at the beach, arms iridescent with cocoa oil, smiles sharp and permanent. Beneath their picture is the same black and white photo of Geoffrey Beldon shown to me by Officer Davies, and another one that shows Geoffrey in handcuffs, being led away by police outside a convenience store in Georgia. There is a short interview with the clerk who recognized him and alerted the authorities. There is an accompanying article which makes mention of a younger sibling who may have inadvertently impeded the investigation.

At the funeral my mother sobs loudly, embarrassingly. She throws her body over Gracie's casket and pounds on the lid with her fists. She has to be helped to the limousine by two assistants from the funeral home, while my father and I walk together, at a distance.

My father holds things together initially. He strokes my hair at night and promises we will all feel better one day. He feeds my mother her sleeping pills and brushes her hair for her when she wakes. When I tell him about my nightmares, he pulls a camping cot out of our garage and brings it into the room I once shared with Gracie. He cannot sleep on Gracie's bed. My mother forbids it.

I trim the hair on Razal's back to a quarter of an inch while he talks on and on about Mrs. Wickham. He tells me that she made an obscene gesture at him just that morning when he brought her a bag of good tomatoes from the fruit stand on Johnson Street.

"A feisty, feisty woman!" he says.

I tell him that the wax will feel warm, and when I spread it across the left flank of his back, he sighs.

"Last chance," I tell him, "Are you sure about this?"

He tells me yes and I smooth a cloth strip along his back. I tell him I'm going to count to three, and then pull.

"Yes," he says, "okay."

His skin breaks out in goose bumps and I can see his muscles flexing involuntarily, little bursts of movement like explosions under his skin. My hands have stopped shaking, but I still don't want to do this. I hate the idea of being responsible for his pain and wonder if he will still come to me once his back has been ripped smooth.

I count to three but instead of pulling right away, I hesitate. Razal sucks in his breath and holds it and I yank the cloth strip free in one quick tug. He doesn't scream or grunt, like many of my clients. I don't even hear him exhale. I ask if he's okay and he replies with a terse yes.

His back has a single swath of smooth skin, with tiny leftover globs of wax clinging to a few hairs around the edges. It looks obscene and coarse, and I'm embarrassed that I am to blame for this.

"Are you sure you want me to continue?" I ask.

"Of course," he says, "this is nothing. Besides, no stopping now." He chuckles when he says this and hitches a thumb over his shoulder at his striped back.

I smear on more wax. He is quiet the rest of the time while I work. Without his stories to fill the spaces between us, the room feels cold. All of its energy converges on Razal's blazing back, the sharp sting and held breath accompanying each pull.

I feel like I should speak. I think about telling him how I once pulled my car into a shady spot across from his apartment complex. From there, I watched for almost an hour while he played cards with his friends. They drank beer and laughed, and once in a while paused to stand up and stretch, or kick a ball back and forth with one of the children.

But of course, I can't tell him this. Nothing else comes, so I remain silent.

When it becomes obvious that my nightmares are not a short-term phenomenon, my father makes an appointment with Dr. Janet, a kindly man with a patient smile and a soft voice. It is Dr. Janet's task to help me accept the death of my sister, and learn how to move forward with my own life. I come to understand that success in this endeavor means my nightmares will have to be eradicated.

At our first meeting, I try to explain my dreams to Dr. Janet, but I get confused and the words tangle up and die around me. Finally, I ask for a piece of paper and a pencil. I draw a line down the center of the paper and title one half "Real Life" and the other half "Dream." I start with the "Real Life" side of the paper, sketching two trees with stick figures outlined flat against the trunks. I write Lucy's name beneath the first tree, Gracie's beneath the second.

I show it to Dr. Janet. He nods.

The "Dream" side of the paper has three nametags. Gracie's name is beneath the first tree, and my own name is beneath the second, taking my sister's factual place. Lucy's name is encapsulated in a bubbly cloud that floats over both trees.

Dr. Janet has enough background on the story to know that Lucy went first. The press made a big deal out of that—how much worse it must have been for Gracie to watch what happened to her best friend, knowing all the while that she would be next.

When I show the "Dream" half of my diagram to Dr. Janet, he pulls at his short white beard, looking puzzled for a moment, before lucidity washes over him. He had already realized what I was seeing each night as I slept was the murder of my sister. What I have to sketch for him is the fact that my vantage point in the dream is the vantage point that belonged to Gracie in real life. So each night, I don't just watch her die. I experience what she experienced. I feel her same grinding fear of being next in line.

After several months of weekly visits with Dr. Janet, it becomes evident that, in spite of his best efforts, he will not be able to end my nightmares. I feel badly that after all his years of study and despite all the certificates and diplomas on his walls, he can't undo a child's bad dreams, even when he desperately wants to. I feel so badly that I eventually tell him my dreams have stopped, but mention that I am getting headaches—a small truth in that large bed of lies. He seems almost giddy as he reaches for his prescription pad and scrawls out a cure.

My mother eventually finds an outlet for her grief. She spearheads a campaign to promote background checks on school employees. She writes letters to several newspaper editors and congressmen. She organizes petitions, and travels to meetings and legislative sessions in different states to tell them her story. Our house becomes another hotel room for her. She stops in two or three times a month to reorganize, then heads back out the door.

There are pieces of her left behind like fossils: her blouses hanging in the closet, a few pairs of shoes lined up along the closet floor, her lipsticks drying out inside her makeup drawer.

My father becomes the parent who signs all my permission forms. He takes me to buy new clothes for school in the fall and drives me to doctor and dentist appointments. Nobody is surprised in my junior year of high school when my parents divorce.

At graduation my mother shows up wearing a purple suit with a green and gold scarf. My father sits next to her in a plain white oxford, his hands dormant in his lap. They seem so different from each other that it is hard to believe they were once married, that they once looked forward to spending weekends together, lounging around in their matching robes.

I move out of the house when I start classes at the Healing Arts Center. It takes me three years to get through my classes and clinics and then, two weeks after I become a licensed massage therapist and esthetician, my father kills himself in his bedroom.

The gun had been purchased several years earlier. Since he never mentioned its existence to me, I assume he had his plans worked out from the beginning, from the moment he made his selection and wrote out the check. The years that followed the purchase were spent waiting.

I imagine him living with the knowledge of his intentions every day. Waking up and wanting it. Considering it. Perhaps even pulling out the gun and handling it, practicing how he would lift it to his temple. Then reconsidering. Enduring his misery for another day because there is a daughter, a living daughter, to think about. There is her education that must be completed, her career that must be decided.

At my father's funeral there are a handful of people from his office and a couple of neighbors, no doubt showing up out of a sense of community. Since Gracie, since the orange groves, our family had stopped having friends over for dinner, and the number of invitations we'd received from others had dwindled as well.

A Federal Express envelope from my mother arrives the day of the funeral, her handwriting almost completely covering a sympathy card inside. She writes that she is sorry she cannot be there, but there are previous commitments from which she cannot extract herself. I read it from beginning to end, knowing that the interviews she has scheduled, the lectures she's promised to give, are a front for the fact that she's closed the book on the part of her life that included my father. The part that included me.

"Stop, please," Razal says suddenly, and I freeze just as I'm about to spread the fourth swath of wax.

"What is it?" I ask, "Are you okay?"

He pushes himself into a sitting position and smiles at the floor.

"Hoo," he says, "Maybe I need a little break."

I pull a clean towel from the cupboard and cover his shoulders.

He sits, slightly hunched, with his hands in his lap.

"You think I am foolish," he says.

"No, of course not." My words fall weak and flat and useless into the room, and I feel certain that if I'm not careful with how I handle things, Razal may never return. Whatever shame or humiliation he feels will keep him from coming back to me. "You're not the first person to need a break," I say, but I don't sound convincing.

He lifts his attention from the floor and stares at the wall. We're both quiet. I know that he is waiting for me to speak, to reassure him. Instead, I offer to turn on the small television.

"It helps," I explain, "to focus your attention on something else."

Razal nods and settles his body back into position. I hand him the remote control and point at the power button. MTV comes on. Most clients who watch television during waxing are young girls. They hum along with the boy bands and move around a lot and I have to ask them to hold still.

Razal looks at the video. A group of curvy women in bikinis, engaged in a squirt-gun fight at a beach. He laughs.

"I think maybe no," he says, sounding a bit more like himself. He presses the channel button and switches through a succession of programs. I tell him I'm going to begin again, that we don't have much longer to go. My back is turned to the television when Razal finally stops changing channels and settles on the local news station.

I don't have to look to know the anchor is talking about Gracie and Lucy. I know there is footage of Geoffrey Beldon, of miles and miles of orange groves, of my sister and her best friend, still here, still staring down at me after all these years.

I mix the wax in slow circles and focus on the consistency, but what I'm thinking about is this little catalogue of tragedy I've been lugging around, the way it tears little bits out of me, then funnels them away. It strikes me how ludicrous it is that I'm stirring wax in this room while a man rests behind me, half-naked, waiting to be made smooth in order to increase his chances with the woman he thinks he loves. I stir and stir and the same things keep swirling around me. My sister in the orange groves. Geoffrey with his baseball bat. My father at my graduation ceremony, staring somewhere past me, guns in his eyes.

Razal clucks his tongue behind me. "A shame," he says, "Such a shame. These girls, they are so young."

I spread the wax along his back. Razal takes a deep breath. His tension is unmistakable.

I feel as if the television is a window and I'm being watched through it. Everyone is watching me perform this absurd act on an old man in love. Lucy, Gracie, Geoffrey, my mother. My father, Dr. Janet, Officer Davies, they're all there, somewhere.

My mother's voice fills the room now. She recites the four steps parents can take to ensure their children's safety. I drop the stirring rod into the wax and watch it sink slowly down. I'm calm as I walk over to the table and take the remote from Razal's hands. He's confused when I flick the power off, just as the image of Lucy and Gracie at Cinderella castle appears onscreen.

"What is it?" he asks, "There is a problem?"

I shake my head and return to spreading wax along Razal. His skin jumps and goose bumps spread along his body.

"That girl," I say. "Gracie."

"The girl on TV. Yes?"

"She was my sister," I tell him, reaching for a cloth strip.

"I am sorry," Razal says, and I know it's true.

I tell Razal everything while I work, startled by the way my story lifts out of me so easily. Razal listens without speaking.

I tell him about the letters I found, then burned. My voice sounds strange and I feel as if I'm listening to my story along with Razal, hearing the events of my life as if they happened to someone else. I smooth the cloth strip over the wax and I'm separated from the events that took place in those orange groves. I'm hearing the story told for the first time.

I place my left hand into the cleft between Razal's shoulders for support. When he reaches his hand over his shoulder and rests his fingertips on mine, it feels as if my entire nervous system rushes to my fingers, receptors firing until my whole arm reverberates with energy. I take a deep breath and walk Razal through the orange groves, pointing out the way the trees go on endlessly, the gaps and chasms in the landscape through which an entire family has disappeared. I tighten my grip on Razal's cloth strip and when I pull it off, he barely flinches.

Christiana Langenberg

In-Coming

The day you hear on the radio about the woman in west Texas who drowned all her children in the bathtub is the day you think about the end of your own rope. You don't have five children under the age of four and you don't have post-partum depression, but somehow you don't think you need all of that to know how she feels. If you funnel the differences between you and her, the one thing that keeps refusing to go through the neck is that she was born with the brain cell that allowed her to do this, and you weren't. There but for the grace of God, go you.

Somebody from the back of the Ride Share van whispers, "Hail Mary, full of grace, the lord is with thee . . ."

The Jewish biologist on your right says, "Wasn't the youngest child's name Sarah, not Mary?"

People are always asking you big questions, in search of small answers. *How are you? How's it going?* As if you know. *How can you take it? What strength do you draw on?* Some people stare at you with faces dimpled as golf balls. *Gosh, what keeps you from letting go of the end of your rope?*

You tell them "Nothing." As in, if you do that, you have nothing, but you know they don't hear it this way.

"If I were you," they go on, their head pivoting left to right on their collective neck, "I couldn't take it. I'd put a gun to my head."

At this point in the conversations you shrug. You must have some sort of immunity.

You know this much. Let go of the end of your rope and you'd go caterwauling into the abyss. You know something else. For you it wouldn't be caterwauling. It would be slow motion, the sound on mute. Like falling headlong and silent, chute-less into the rest of your life.

You know some of the really awful things aren't the big loud events; they're happenings small as microbes. You think even the Virgin Mary must have found herself reduced to one inane thing following another. Maybe it was the mindless sweeping of Jesus hairs that fell from his head every day. Or her reflection in the river where she beat her and Joseph's garments against rocks; there she could tell that light blue wasn't really her color. She might even have said on occasion, "I'm sick of tidying up the place while he's out turning bread and sardines into a buffet for thousands. This is not the life I imagined for myself." Then she'd take the sheets off the line and fold them into beatific squares.

Or something like that. The accumulation of resentment too often looks like the certainty of coping.

So when people offer you Jesus as an elixir for your life, it goes somewhat cottony in your mouth. The first therapist you saw after the funeral said, "It's really no miracle or mystery. Some things are just plain hard to swallow."

So now you have a plan you follow religiously, if you will. You put up your hand between you and the random well-wisher, and, in your best Diana Ross and the Supremes voice, suggest, "Stop in the name of love, before you break my heart. Think it oh over." And they do. They twitch or retract their arms from the ready-to-hug position and stop.

You stand there calm as a crossing guard. They laugh nervously and you don't. You're at the end of your rope, and you know by now it is best not to fidget. It throws odd shadows on the wall.

Out in the yard one day you step on something that crackles. You push aside the poppies, see a snakeskin coiled tight as a lasso, and stare at it as if it's a vaccine for cancer. *God damn*, you think. *What a great idea!* Exfoliate your thin skin and get another better suited to the climate you're facing. After all, you have had it. You are so full, so up to here with tragedy, that something has to give. If you could lose the thin skin, you think, the hair-trigger on your emotional catapult, for crying out loud, then you'd lose the shackles of grief. It makes perfect sense.

Maybe second-degree sunburn would help speed things along. You adjust the chaise lounge into the oncoming path of noon rays and promptly fall asleep until the neighbor's dog Kiki licks the sweat from your toes.

In the shower, the water on your chest feels like hot wax. It's your body against a thing too hot to touch but impossible to pull away from. You hum into the spray of water the way she used to say, "Mr. Sandman, bring me a dream" into the breeze from the box fan in the window, her laughter thudding into the pillows under your head.

Trying to say her name aloud is like trying to haul a dumb waiter up 100 stories with your vocal cords. You can not do it. The sound just won't travel vertically. You decided one night that if you didn't say her name at all, her entire image would vaporize less. You'd wake up tomorrow and there'd be less of her gone.

It's a neat trick you've been pulling off, that's for sure. You go to sleep in your room and wake up in hers, unable to account for how that happened to be. The therapist says it's hard to believe you sleepwalk, rational as you are. Yet there you are mornings, feet angled under the stuffed hedgehog collection, some of them still wearing the boas made out of maxi pads. You wonder when, if ever, you'll feel like putting things away.

It seems almost silly to keep the high-rise apartment building she constructed out of Kleenex boxes. For nearly a year now, Popsicle stick people have reclined on washcloth couches under a thin layer of accumulating dust.

Moments like this you feel you could actually crumple, your skin only a tent of bed sheets and broom handles leaning precariously in on each other. You think of your internal organs as doll-sized and hollow, all the room inside you diminished to maybe one errant brain stem cell that just doesn't know any better but to keep on firing. You feel so small inside, the cartography of your bones visible in fluorescent lighting. You've been avoiding all forced air vents and have put duct tape over the switches for ceiling fans to keep from being scattered by that final, unexpected exhaust.

The way out dawns on you when you are getting your Hepatitis booster. Vaccinate yourself against tragedy.

Because you had a life sciences minor, you understand the basic principle of this. Get your body to recognize the enemy and build antibodies against it. Take on other people's tragedies in microscopic form. Molecules of tragedies, you tell yourself, only tiny bits. All you want is a vaccine to prevent whatever is coming next from getting into your life. You have to stop it from consuming you like some kind of flesh-eating bacteria.

After your daughter's death, you stopped getting sick. You never got the flu again, and when other people were crippled by colds, hunched into Kleenexes and over aromatic teas, you wore tank tops in winter and forgot how to spell echinasea. Brazen white blood cells patrolled your veins.

But now it turns out your own stubborn, vibrant health is like a sneer in the mirror. Nobody else sees how it makes you wonder who you are. Maybe you missed something. Maybe there's a stone you left unturned, something more to know.

The sperm bank is sorry, but they cannot reveal the donor's identity; they simply have to rely on truthful self-reporting of family medical histories for cancer, and with this donor there was none. Um, the donor was 25 at the time of collection. There was some asthma, she reminds you, and a sibling with a possible peanut allergy. "Those can be life-threatening," she says, like this is a party favor.

What you need is about 10 cc of some completely objective tragedy. Someone else's undoing, for a change, a pain entirely removed from you as if grown in a petri dish clear across town. Something you didn't want and can't have and won't get.

Here is what you'll do. First thing in the morning you will snag the very corner of the first thing that takes your breath away. Start with the obvious. Skip the part where you open your eyes to daylight, the sky wide open just outside your window. Instead, keep your eyes closed when you resurface. Find the doorway, grope your way down the stairs, feel the wall along the stairwell until you get to the bottom. Then walk like Frankenstein, at a diagonal with your arms stretched out, before you get to the front door. Open it and nudge around for the newspaper with your foot. Bend down and bring it up to your face as you roll the rubber band down its inky, smudged back. Snap it open.

The headline news. Just what you need. *Mother, four children—10, 8, 6, 5—brutally murdered. Boyfriend in custody.* There is a glamour photo of the dead woman, the one they will show on the evening news later, the one they will put on top of the casket, where she is smiling and looking out the tops of her eyes as if she has years left in her to break the hearts of a series of men. She is dead now at what would've been your age five years ago.

Too close. Don't read the whole story, just culture the details from the picture. Change it to one taken at a family picnic the day before, where you imagine the woman in her backyard wearing a shirt with a button missing, the fourth one down, maybe, the one she meant to sew on after ironing, but the first few neighbors were already over for the barbecue, and she was standing at the ironing board in her bra, so she just put the damn shirt on. That shirt. One with a ketchup stain 20 minutes later just to the right of the third button. The ketchup from the mouth of her youngest, the five year old, about to start kindergarten, who kissed her there on that shirt after she excused herself from the rest of her hot dog, into the last six hours of her life. No make that 8-10 hours. It says the boyfriend allegedly shot her after the kids went to bed.

You are having no reaction. Good. It might be working. Find another headline. *Drive-by shooting kills 9 month old in family kitchen.* There is a photo of an empty walker in front of a refrigerator with an alligator magnet on it.

Honeymooning couple attacked by shark, groom feared dead. Big surprise, you think. What next.

Farm accident rips arms off budding violinist.

Stuff that makes other people's body temperature drop, or call in sick to work, hug their children more often, this doesn't even make you blink. *Accidents happen*, you think.

You drift out the back door, sit in the sun, and nearly levitate in the chaise. You've got to love immunity. You feel nothing but your skin heating up, slowly darkening. Kiki smiles at you through the hole in the fence.

One month later, you're at the credit union and still symptom-free. You're in line for the next available teller, whose voice is coming from behind a giant tissue pumpkin." Can I help the next person in line?" and you're thinking she probably can't. Another teller you *can* see has done something truly awful to her hair. You're wondering how long it takes her to look like that, when you hear a girl, the young girl who has budged in front of you and is talking to another eye-lined teenage girl.

"So my boyfriend's parents are being really nice about everything and they're going to give me part of his ashes."

"Freaky," says her friend.

You look at her directly, at the tufts of pink hair escaping her beige bandana and you ask, "Ashes? Your boyfriend's ashes? He's dead?"

"Uh huh." She nods. "Two weeks ago." She looks so serene, she could be ceramic and wearing a light blue robe and standing with palms open among somebody's zinnias.

"Is your name Mary?" you ask. Two weeks ago. Jesus Christ.

She shakes her head just like a real girl.

"Could you please pass me a deposit slip?" You gesture toward the black plastic slot in front of her on the counter.

What she says next is either "car accident" or "bar accident" or maybe even "tar accident," but you have already stopped listening.

Your hand is up. Stop. In the. Before you. My heart.

You try to decide what is really tragic here. The single-sized serving of the dead boyfriend, or your dwarfed emotional reaction where you should be having none at all. You tidy up the stack of deposit slips and jiggle the pencil holder to settle the pens and pencils into the bottom of the matching cup. Look at how stunned she is. A dead boyfriend. Her life is starting over and she's sluggish out of the blocks.

You take the deposit slip and pretend to be writing something valid on it, but then she says it. She names him "Andy—" before you can clamp your ears shut again and you watch your hand write *1/4 C of Andy* on your check stub. You see fine powdery boyfriend dust in an acrylic measuring cup.

You look at the girl who strikes you, suddenly, as an emotional anorexic. She is pale as notebook paper and doesn't rustle much when the breeze from the oscillating fan waves by. You wonder if she has considered sprinkling some of Andy on her toast every morning, like cinnamon sugar, to somehow digest what is happening. If she went lightly, he could last for quite some time.

The teller raises her voice, "NEXT?!"

You lurch forward and drop your wallet. "I need to withdraw. I need to make a withdrawal," you say.

"But this is a deposit slip," she answers, smiling, "Care for some candy corn?" and she pushes a little cellophane packet toward you with *You're Business is Sweet* written on it.

"The thing is," you tell her. " I don't know how much I can take."

"We're only allowed to give one treat per customer." She smiles more insistently.

"Never mind," you mutter. You can hardly believe your bank is trick-or-treating. "I want to deposit half of this," and you push your check forward, cram the cash she hands you into your pocket. Christ almighty. Treats at a time like this.

Outside you look around at everything that was familiar before you stepped into the bank. Now you feel like whistling for your car. Maybe it'll come galloping to you from wherever the hell it has parked itself. Who's that saint you're supposed to pray to when you lose things? Oh you forgot, you don't pray.

On your second trip back down the block you see the boyfriendless teenager sitting in the passenger seat of a blotchy orange Vega. There is nobody in the driver's seat. It looks like a sunset, diagonally parked.

She looks used to waiting. You stare at her and she stares back, her eyes heavy in her face like a bassett hound.

Without knowing why or expecting to understand later, you walk over to her side of the car, rummage around in your pockets and clamp half your cash, along with the first grade picture of your daughter from your wallet under the windshield wiper. She is wearing the itchy sweater you made her wear because your mother spent $75 on the wool, and by God she was going to wear it at least once if Nana worked that hard to make it. You had also made her turn off the TV so she could finish her breakfast and have time to brush her teeth before school. "It's almost over," she'd whined. "You won't miss a thing," you'd promised. In the picture she looks like she is prepared to be sad for the rest of her life.

There is nothing else to say. Not even this.

You wish for the teenage girl that instead of an accident that extinguished her boyfriend into a pile of ashes, it might have been a natural disaster, say a tornado. That he might have been sucked up into a funnel cloud and blended with the side of a barn and then rained down upon her like confetti. That she might have a piece of his femur embedded in her skull, instead of his whatever in a jar. She needs something hair can grow over or be combed against it. He should be something she won't have to explain to future lovers unless she absolutely wants to. Ashes of Andy on the mantel are hard to ignore.

On the drive home you accidentally run over a cat and all the time, in your rear view mirror, you think it is just a tire, just a piece of a tire, somebody's lone athletic shoe, something black, a black tumble, end over end. Until you are able to make out arms.

In the middle of the night you flip on the light in the bathroom because you have to pee and there is a dark mass against the lime green of the rug. Instinctively you raise the small plastic garbage can full of tampon casings and smash the thing. It turns out to be the hugest cricket you've ever seen in your life. Its hind leg remains behind in the shag of the carpet as you lift its carcass with a Kleenex. It is a huge hind leg. It could feature as a close second to one of those barbecued turkey legs they sell at the state fair. The turkey legs you cannot bring yourself to eat, ever since you saw that one cartoon of double amputee frogs in wheelchairs, working the kitchen of a gourmet restaurant where the specialty is frog legs. Or the greeting card of the boneless chicken ranch, where boneless chickens are scattered around the hills like polka dots.

You used to think these things were funny, now you just get back into bed, pull the covers up to your neck and shiver yourself into something that approximates sleep.

I t is Thursday and the deposit slip with *1/4 cup of Andy* on it is still tucked in your pocket from Monday. Why didn't you recycle it with the newspaper, or trade it in for the 19 year old who ran the stop sign and was broadsided after leaving his parents' anniversary party? Or the triplets who were all three killed when a semi-truck rear-ended the family's van? Or the yet one more ex-husband who violated a restraining order and shot his ex-wife dead before turning the gun on himself.

Turn on the radio. Some early morning Djs are interviewing a comic from the Me Generation whose routine includes this question, "No seriously, what's the worst way to die?" Something besides the obvious is all wrong about this.

You pull open the bottom drawer of that green lacquered armoire that was huge when you were a child and now looks like a Barbie wardrobe. There is the squashed pink shoebox with random photos in it, and there is your daughter standing on that rock at the edge of Lake Superior with the spray of the next wave still two seconds away from giving her the shock of her life. That was before, way before Stage IV neuroblastoma meant anything to either one of you. Far before it mattered at all that Herbert Hoover's grave is just a stone's throw from Baby Me Me, what she used to call herself when she couldn't say her name. Funny that now Herbert has become your landmark to Me instead of the other way around. Funny too how all these people walk around breathing and you're still waiting for her to exhale, before that last time she didn't. You often wonder where that last pocket of air is holed up. "Hey, Me," is the only thing you say when you go to visit her down the row from Herbert.

I t's Pam's turn to drive the Ride Share van and because she is always cold, she has the heat on and the fan turned to blow-dry. Camille is in the front seat. "Jesus Christ, Pam, I can feel my bangs baked onto the back of my neck. Can we turn the fucker off?"

"I wish you wouldn't use the lord's name in vain," says Albert.

"Prophet's name," says Sarah from the back seat.

"I'm not using it in vain," Camille responds. "I have a definite reason. Turn the fucking heat down!"

"Middle ground, people," says Sarah. "Let's find some middle ground."

Albert turns up the volume on the small TV he brings with him every morning and plugs into the cigarette lighter. It's enough to make you want to smoke. He doesn't want to miss a thing.

The morning news anchor, the one who looks like an adult version of your daughter with her smooth brown hair and the cowlick in the same place in her hairline, is reporting a road rage incident where some woman's poodle was flung into traffic by the irate motorist who cut her off.

There is a still photo of a man shrugging outside the police station and suddenly your heart rate hammers in your ears. He is being released on his own recognizance, wearing his unruffled malice like a badge. He shrugs his shoulders, takes a hit off an inhaler and holds his breath.

Your aortic valve opens wide. Your heart empties itself, blood rushes to all your extremities, makes them so very heavy, impossible to flail. Your throat fills with bile.

"Stop the van," you tell Pam.

"It's a green light, Sleepy," she says.

"Just stop. Stop! I need to get out. I'm going to be sick."

She looks at you in the rear view mirror, and puts her blinker on, eases over onto the shoulder. You don't even like poodles.

Albert opens the door quickly and you get out just as the anchor is saying, " . . . a wrongful death suit has been filed against the man allegedly responsible for the poodle's death."

"I'll be fine," you lie and slide the door between you and Albert's worried look. "Just go on. I'll walk the rest of the way."

The van pulls away slowly, all 12 pairs of eyes inside watching you walk over to the picnic table chained to the north side of this ice cream stand. Frost thick as upholstery covers the bench, still you sit on it. Chances are you won't be able to feel anything other than what you're feeling anyway. The sign in the window says, "Sweetie's is closed for the season. Please come again."

You lift each of your 100-pound hands up to your head and swallow over and over until the sunrise is done. You manage not to vomit by controlling your breathing. This takes the good part of forever.

So much for immunity.

Two days later in a restaurant a guy at the table behind you is relating the road rage story to the other guy he's having lunch with. He is laughing as if he can't help himself. He says "So I guess the guy reaches in and grabs the chick's dog—y'know, one of those yappy ones and—get this—throws it . ." he pauses to laugh some more, "into traffic and the damn thing gets run over."

A voice comes from somewhere inside you that's done with keeping quiet. At first it doesn't feel at all right. It is like trying to get out of your clothing in the deep end of the pool so that you can pass Life Saving 101. Or maybe it's heavier than wet denim and harder to maneuver.

You wonder if this is what deaf people sound like to themselves, saying a thing just to say it, knowing they can't hear.

You turn around and stare. The storyteller looks at you but does not pick up on your fiercely hoisted eyebrows. "Excuse me!?" you begin and fling your look at the side of his head. It ricochets off his temple and pings around the restaurant. "Ex-CUSE me?!"

His head turns. His eyes rub you out. He hands you the ketchup and keeps talking.

"No," you say. "The poodle. Pass the poodle, you stupid fuck!"

He looks at you over the sandwich he is collapsing into his mouth. Still his expression doesn't change.

"You think road rage is funny, Asshole?"

He rolls his eyes. There is mayonnaise, like hydrophobia, at the edge of his lip.

You lean toward him and hiss. "Let me reach inside *your* car and toss your kid into traffic. Let's watch his braces puncture the tires of an SUV. Let's shrug about that."

He eyes appear to wiggle. "Lady," he says. "It's a dog."

"Which is more than I can say for you, you fuck," you answer.

The guy's friend at the table frowns. "Ben, let it go," he whispers.

"What? I'm wrong?" you ask him. He shakes his head. You stand up and ask the whole restaurant. "What, I'm wrong?" Nobody answers. "What about the person who *loved* the dog? You think about that?!"

Somehow you manage to score six weeks disability leave from work. Your reason is that you are too sad to work. You call in sad to work. This alarms everyone because not only are you never sick, but you are never sad. What you do not tell them is something that's been true for so long it has displaced your entire history. *There is more sadness in me than there even is me.* You know if you say this the secretary will flip out.

To her you cannot say, "Look Corinne, everything finally got to me," because you already know she counts on this not being true. She would keep her mouth in a thin straight line while your words hung between you. She would wait for you to make a lame joke. She would wait for your next move. She would have the patience for this.

Then she would say, "So back to where we were. How do I code that? Is this a personal day or a vacation day?"

You leave her a message on her voice mail. "Corinne, I'm sad. I'm taking a sick day."

After two weeks, when you're sure nobody will be there, you stop in at 6:00 to look over your mail with no intention whatsoever of opening a goddamn thing. Corinne stands up from behind the main desk where she is giving the plants haircuts. She rewinds the long strands of ivy around the macramé hanger, snips the air next to the bromeliad, clears her throat and walks past you with the aloe to a new spot in the west window. "Uh, please provide a doctor's note for why you're still out," she says as she passes, staring intently at the vermiculite in front of her.

The lid to the trash can doesn't squeak when you push it open wide enough for your stack of envelopes. They land on a neat pile of leaves. "Sure thing." You've got 1,863 sick time hours you've never used.

This is no problem. You've spent two of these six weeks of leave volunteering at the hospital, job shadowing various medical personnel. They have tasks they complete. You admire this. They, unlike you, don't stall between the toothbrush and the toothpaste, water running unchecked down the drain. You liken them to super heroes and imagine them with capes on.

They find you odd. Oddly antiseptic. And they mean your personality.

The phlebotomist lets you help with the femoral artery draw on a comatose patient. She tells you she could lose her job, but you answer, "Like he's going to talk?"

"Have you accepted Jesus into your life?" she asks you.

Because you are not making eye contact, you can't tell if she is serious. You are palpating this guy's vein, looking for a pulse in his inner thigh. You can't be thinking about Jesus. "Look at all the people who've lost Jesus and end up finding him at the laundromat." You shrug. "Jesus is like lint."

"That is sick," she says.

"That's the point," you answer. "Everyone here is sick. I'm camouflaging."

She looks puzzled and she's wearing too much dark purple eye shadow. Her face wrinkles up like a prune. "You're a sicko," she repeats and gives your shoulder a little tap. She stretches her mouth into a temporary smile. "I hope you know that."

This makes you wish she were highly contagious. Hope. That single syllable cannonball toward the future. Hope. Now there's optimism. Reality-based hope is probably like a religious experience. Hope that's not blind, that isn't wavering on pure bullshit, anything to keep you from pitching brain-first into despair.

You are walking that serrated edge, the one between laughing and weeping. You're on a recumbent emotional stairmaster. How many steps so far today?

Maybe all of this, your whole adult life, is a long dark joke, inching itself toward a punch line you can't imagine. Your therapist sighs and says, "Try to remember—all's well that ends well." That might be, but it's taking too long to get to the point where you laugh without echoing.

You've been reassigned to an ultrasound tech who says she heard you have a weird sense of humor. She has a funny story to tell you. Once when she first started, she told a pregnant woman who had her head turned toward the wall, "There are two heads," when it was really two distinct people, twins, on the screen. Everybody laughed afterwards, especially later, after the one twin's heart surgery was successful and the mother was told the infant could expect to lead a reasonably normal life. "Better than a two-headed baby," the sonographer says, the same way other people say, "Better than a jab in the ass with a sharp stick." She elbows you for effect.

But you don't laugh. You think of the two-headed blue monster on the "Sesame Street" show, the one who converses between its two heads in honks and squeaks, the one your daughter thought was way too scary, even though she knew it was designed to make her laugh.

You imagine the fallout in that pregnant woman's skull the moment the tech said, "See? Here's one head, there's the other" without adding that there were an equal number of bodies to match. She must have thought, even for the briefest moment, that she was having a two-headed baby.

Don't disbelieve the unbelievable, you're always telling yourself. A mortality rate of 1.2 per 100,000 means everything if you're the 1.2. It isn't as if 100 story buildings can't melt like cheap candles, or monster waves can't extinguish hundreds of thousands of lives. Tragedy is forever going to try and best itself.

The mother of the multi-baby was a non-native speaker of English, which somehow adds to the humor of the story for the sonographer telling it. She is wearing a small button on her white lapel. It reads *United We Stand*. "The woman's English was very good," she manages to add.

Still, you know the mother must not have understood. She had every reason not to. The thing maybe she cannot forget is what her first thought was. *I cannot have one babies. I cannot live this nightmare.*

Of course, she didn't have a two-headed baby. She had two babies, but for the very long moment that it was a two-headed baby, she had a valid reason to fear what her life had become. But then it was two whole babies and she was twice blessed, not twice damned. But once the fear was lit within her, it never fully extinguished. Some things you can't unhear.

Nobody ever says twice damned. You think maybe somebody should.

The sonographer is waiting for you to laugh. "Two heads. How much baby?" she repeats.

You unbutton your lab coat and show her your t-shirt *This is What a Radical Feminist Looks Like.*

"I'll bet you're lots of fun at parties," she answers and pops in a new tape. "Next patient has an AWOL testicle," she continues. "Urologist wants me to find it. Ten bucks says it's holed up in the canal." She locks eyes with you.

"I've got a quarter," you answer. "But you're the pro."

"Lighten up, Honey." She shakes her head. "We've got a small room and a long, long day here."

You get reassigned to Radiology where you actually like the feel of the lead apron. It's familiar somehow, comfortable, even. You also enjoy the way everyone but the patient has to step out of the room, the satisfying buzz of the X-ray machine, like a correct answer on Jeopardy. But the best part of all is the relief on people's faces when they hear something inside is broken, and their simultaneous belief that it can be fixed.

This is how you vaccinate yourself against tragedy.
    Never get born.
    The only sure way to avoid contracting tragedy is if the possibility of you assigns itself to slow-swimming sperm or if the potential for you is actually an egg with a particularly impermeable membrane.
    A lot of good that does you now. "I never asked to be born," you told your mother when you were 13.
    "That," she answered, "is a flat out lie. I used a diaphragm. And a bucket of spermicide and you lived through that just fine. This right here—" you can still feel her index finger rapping on your collar bone "—is the life you just HAD to have. I figure you got everything coming to you after you insisted on getting here."

This is what happens when things that shouldn't get said, do. They resonate, like auditory tattoos and become the mindless dance steps you have to complete, as you lie sandwiched in the sheets in the mornings, before you get out of bed. You have become a person who steps back, braces herself for everything, then toes the future to see if it shifts or lurches. You approach *Do you want fries with that?* or *We Interrupt This Broadcast to Bring you Breaking News* with the same hedged response. "Maybe."
    Then you take whatever you get.

"I remember you from the E.R.," says the hospital Volunteer Coordinator, whose name is, not surprisingly, Ms. Place. She has asked to see you after your first day with the radiology tech.
    "I haven't been in the E.R. yet," you answer.
    She has a delicate face and looks at you with opalescent blue eyes. "I mean when you were in with your daughter, a couple of years ago. Her name is Claire?"
    You stare at her. At her garnet lipstick.
    She waits.
    "She died."
    Ms. Place nods. "I remember. Her name is still Claire, right?"

Now you nod. "True enough."

"Well one thing I've learned from working here," she says, "besides remembering people's names, is that pain is relative. So is joy."

You nod again. After all, who can argue with that. "Excuse me, Ms. Place, but am I here for a lesson?"

She smiles. "I'm sorry, no. We need help in the neonatal unit. Specifically with the babies who are born with addictions. They need a lot of body contact, a lot of rocking."

"I like Radiology. It works for me." You smack your lips in a satisfied "Yup." You don't want to have to remind her that you're volunteering your time, after all; you're doing *them* a favor.

"I appreciate that, "she tells you, "but we actually need you more in Neonatal."

"I'm not looking to replace my daughter, Ms. Place." You drive your chapstick around your mouth like a pace car. At this point you can sniff out a do-gooder from a mile away.

"And I'm not suggesting that," she answers. "The infants need to be held whether you do it or not. And to be honest—" Her smile widens. "They don't require the same social skills that the adult patients do. You don't even have to speak."

A noise comes out of you that you recognize as a laugh, though it sounds like the whicker of a mule. "Well, thank God for small favors." You shift in your chair. "So. What would I be doing?"

"Just some skin-to-skin holding, rocking, mindless humming. Hearing your heartbeat helps them sleep better. Things like that." She stands up and extends her hand, which is warm and steady. "They'll train you. I'm sure it'll work out," she says, "Really. You'll be pleasantly surprised."

"We'll see," you answer. After all, you don't want to promise anything.

You walk to the back Exit, the one adjacent to the Emergency Room entrance, and wait to put your coat on until you can gauge the weather through the long glass doors. You might not need it, but when the sky is clear at night, the temperature can drop rapidly. It is almost dusk.

Something about the whoosh of the doors opening and closing and the going from warm air to cool is oddly soothing. The Valet Parking teenager stands up to get your car, but you tell him you'll walk.

Somewhere somebody is burning something sweet. It moves past your nose slowly. Leaves, maybe, or the last steak on the grill until spring. This is what you like about the way Indian summer concedes to fall. The attenuated length of light, the world tucking itself in.

You put your coat on, slip your hands into each opposing sleeve, wait to cross the street until the signal changes. You could turn and look up at the fourth floor windows, where the OB floor is, but you'll see it soon enough tomorrow. Right now there are other things to note.

For example, the way one color shields or bears another. With lavender behind it, the oak tree missing half its leaves is less a dark thing. A tangerine smudge on distant hilltops presses the last of daytime into night. Maybe, if you're lucky, there will be hoar frost in the morning, branches blunt with milky tassels too compelling not to touch.

Chris Sheehan

Roots and Limbs

So these poor people living in the house Lane kept up in Willits, their sewer had given out a few months ago, and something *had* happened, keeping us from making the drive, the kind of thing you'd like to tell your buddies, drinking beer in the dump truck, or at the bar, or on your porch. Maybe it's enough to say someone died, or someone's heart stuck in our last trench, someone you don't know, and Lane and I'd found a nice place to sit, just off the Shakespeare exit in Berkeley, where a broad swath of thistle and wheat-grass had been cleared for parking. So yes, we had our own underground construction company—Sewer Connection, we called ourselves—but we weren't the type of characters you wanted showing up on your doorstep. I know I'd send myself away. I know I wouldn't pay however many thousands of dollars for us to work on your home. But like I said, we replaced sewers. It's the kind of work people have a fair amount of sympathy for. You'd be surprised how much business we turned away, even with Lane handling the customers, in whatever voice they gave his mild Tourette's.

If you want to know, Lane had run codes in the Coast Guard, or maybe it was the Air Force, but that's how he put it. They're all the same anyway. It could've been the Navy. He'd done that and something to do with having access to nuclear missiles, if you believe that. But he was a savant of sorts, and I didn't learn much about the service in the Marines, before I broke my kneecap to get out, honorably somehow, which is just a long and embarrassing story of its own, and I'd rather not get into my childhood, and all of the other reasons I ended up there.

Like I said, I'm not the kind of guy you want showing up on your doorstep. And I know Lane's not. I know why he was in the service, too. But I promised him I'd never tell anyone else, not even my son. Some things you have no choice but to hold close to your heart, as they say. What I *can* tell you is he was from a different generation and had spent a year or two running in the same circle as the Hell's Angels, and he'd won a few arm-wrestling championships in Petaluma, where they have a little bronze statue of two guys locked up along their main street. I know this because he drove us by it once, when we happened to be in the general area.

It just happens Willits was where we ended up that day, and I remember driving under the town sign arched over the highway as Lane said, It all seems *Fuck it* smaller, it all seems smaller. Isn't that what everyone says *Fuck it?*

Here, milkweed grew sparsely from the front yard out to the rail's ballast, thickening along the vacant lots near the switchyard and the mill, where steam rose over the house, gripping in the still air. Far off, the ridgeline rifted down and the depressions, slumped on the green-cleared hills, showed rigid in the foggy light.

Don't make it up here much *Fuck it*, he said.

A few doe moved out from the oak scrubs and picked their way across the tracks, toward the overgrown lots. He sat still and watched the deer, his wrist on the wheel, shaking with the idle. Then he shut the diesel down and opened the door.

I need a few more beers, I said. I'm not ready.

He closed the door and sat back in his seat. *Fuck it.* Fine by me. I didn't *Fuck it* plan on working today. Just wanted *Fuck it* make sure you weren't.

A few beers turned into a few more.

Eventually, as the sky broke to a light mist we decided to get out and at least see what the line looked like. We set up the camera at the cleanout by the house. It couldn't have been more than a thirty foot run, and if it was shallow enough, we could pull a new one through in two or three hours. But the line was still full. Typically, if there's grade, even an eighth of an inch per foot, the liquids, or whatever you want to call them, will slowly seep through the blockage. The monitor, an old wood-paneled television, went black a few feet in. We ran that camera all the way until we were clearly in the city main. Even with the debris on the lens we could see a little light in the eight-inch city sewer. The line was flat.

We'd pulled flat lines before—our ethics seemed to vary day to day. We knew it worked well enough to outlive any warranty we slapped on it. But Lane owned this house. In a year or two he'd have the same problem. I'll spare you the details about ejection pumps and so forth and all the codes involved, and just say I didn't feel up to open-trenching this line into the street. It was the kind of job we liked to run away from, screaming.

I put the camera in the truck's bed, then set the monitor in the back cab and fastened the seat belt around it. There's nothing we can do *today*, I said. I opened a beer and watched him wrap the extension cord over his shoulder, shaking a little more than normal. His case was mild, like I said. There was nothing out of the ordinary about him unless you got close enough to hear his tick or study his hands, though once he'd told me he didn't know what he said when he lost control of himself. I know what he said around me, but I'm sure I was the only person he'd ever asked.

He wrapped the cord tightly in a professional way, then set it in the bed and pulled out a shovel. Let me *Fuck it* know when you're ready *Fuck it* to start fusing the pipe. *Fuck it* I'll dig this one. He walked to the property line, where dirt gave to the sidewalk, and started digging.

I'm not the kind of person who can watch someone work. Neither of us were. Like I said, this wasn't a city operation. I'm also not the kind of person who likes working for no reason. You don't need to understand the particulars to know this wasn't the best solution. Honestly, we only pulled flat lines when the customer didn't have money to do anything else. We tried our best to lay it all out for them, explain how the earth moves, how roots aren't too picky about their nutrients—how shit likes to flow down hill.

But he wouldn't let me in the hole. Every few minutes he'd ask for the saw, or a new blade, or to plug the cord back in. There were roots, and the shovel wasn't doing much good. He tried for a while with a pick. He tried loosening the soil with the little roto hammer, but there wasn't much soil around the roots. I wasn't going to be a part of this, I remember deciding. I took what beer was left from the truck and sat down on the porch. But just then a man stepped out next door and lit a cigarette. There's always an old man coming out to talk.

He walked to the side, where a gravel drive ran into the backyard and I could see his RV parked in the thistle. He stood a time, studying the mill, as if somehow he'd never seen it before, then he walked to the porch and held out his hand. Usually, I'd be drinking out of a coffee cup and lighting a cigarette, but we weren't getting paid for this job. Paul, I said. It's good to meet you, Frank.

I offered him a beer.

The old lady, he said, and nodded to the near window, where the shades were cracked against the light. Oh, what the hell, he said. You only live once, he said. I can't remember the last time I said that. He was tall, thin, and bald, and he seemed to want to cover his face when he took a drag from his cigarette. She won't leave me alone about this, he said, and knocked on the siding. What are you digging up, there?

A lateral, I said. The sewer's broken.

Those roots will get you every time, he said. We just had ours replaced, must be a year now. You can see where the roots brought up our walk, here, he said, and walked toward Lane, where he followed the roots to his property. Damn things, I don't know where they came from. Not a tree around, I can see. Boy, he's onto something there, he said. That boy's digging to China.

Lane stopped then and turned toward us, breathing heavily. I thought *no* I recognized you, he said. But I don't. *No*, then he went back to the roots.

Where you two from? he said. She's one hell of a truck, he said, and then put his hands on the rack, looking into the bed. You boys use cast iron, he said, and held up a forty-five degree fitting. I hear ABS is the new thing now.

I crushed my can on the sidewalk, then threw it into the bed. I could hear it hit against a few other empties. We don't use plastic, I said.

This here looks like plastic, he said, and pulled down on the pipe, strapped to the rack.

You could run a truck over it, I said. He didn't need to know what it was made of or how we fused it—he didn't need to know anything except we wouldn't be around for more than a few hours. I wanted the guy to leave. I wanted to drink beer on the porch. I wanted to go home and get out of the rain. Like I said, I never dealt with clients. Neither of us liked people, they just responded better to Lane. It was getting late, too. We weren't getting home for dinner, I could tell that much. I knew I'd have to give the wife a call. At some point I'd have to find a pay phone. When we first started we'd had cell-phones, but I got frustrated with mine and threw it out the window, driving down the freeway. So we figured they were a bad investment. It's possible she would have called me twenty times by now. We would have talked about nothing twenty times already. We would have said *I love you* twenty times.

I saw that screen of yours, he said. From a fair distance, he said, nodding again to the facing window. He set his empty beer in the bed. She's been watching the whole time, you know, he said. But you can't blame her. Inside don't look any better than a shit line. You boys are just here to do your job, you don't want to hear about all that. *I* know. I should go in, anyway. She's probably worried about me catching cold.

I was quiet. I waited for the blinds to turn. Then I asked Lane what the fuck was taking so long.

Fuck it there used to be a big oak, Lane said. *Fuck it* old man burned out his clutch trying to pull the stump. He was out of breath and sweating heavily through his Wranglers and undershirt. *Fuck it* there's roots and *Fuck it* there's limbs. I can't *Fuck it* tell the difference. *Fuck it*, he twitched, *Fuck it*, holding the shovel tightly against his chest. Then he used it to step up the foot or so he'd gotten down and took a seat in the wet grass. It was raining steadily now. He ran his hands through his red hair thinned along the sides. You don't ever expect *Fuck it* this *Fuck it* to happen to you, he said. *Fuck it* I should have hired someone *Fuck it*. He stood up then and walked in circles around the yard, as if explaining something to himself, before he sat down on the porch and looked off toward the tracks stretched through the narrow ravine, pulling into the dark cut, his hands still moving on him.

I picked up the shovel, sunk in the mud, and started digging. If this means anything, there *is* an art to digging. I'm not a big guy and somehow this was a source of pride for me. You won't hear that from many people, I know. But these roots split like a sapling, like a madrone sapling, or any other hardwood. I went at them with the narrow shovel—the sharp-shooter, we called it—until my calluses were blistered and raw. I didn't like using anything electric when I dug. I kept at it until light had pulled down the ridge and backed a thin shadow across the yard, the tracks, the house.

In the distance the mill lights lit steam off the tall stacks. I watched the steam hold in the rain while I tried to catch my breath. I watched for what seemed a long time before I lit a cigarette and looked around for Lane. There were a few lights on inside the house.

I climbed out of the hole and looked into it. From above, it looked deep. I remember how deep it seemed. It seemed as if I'd dug twelve feet. But it was dark. And the shovel's handle was still above ground. I snapped the shovel over my knee and set it into the hole. It looked better. I lit another cigarette. I was still out of breath but something about digging made me want to smoke. I remembered a liquor store just off the highway. I thought I should give Lane some time alone. I had an idea about tomorrow, maybe driving up *early*. I was done digging. I was sure about that. I didn't have anything left in me. And I hadn't eaten anything since last night. But I was past the point of eating. I needed to get hydrated and see how things fell into place.

Outside the liquor store there was a pay phone. I had two quarters in change. I dialed home and my son answered. He was twelve. He was doing homework. I could hear the wife yelling in the background. She wanted him to get back to the table so they could finish doing his homework. I told her it'd be a late one. I said this job is kicking our ass. I said it's just another nightmare job. I didn't tell her where we were. I didn't want to get into specifics. Any source of logic I'd had about coming up here was lost on me by now. I didn't know where to start. I told her not to wait up for me. I said it's possible we'll work through the night and sleep in the trailer. We didn't bring the trailer. But it was something we'd done before when we'd work on restaurants. I just hoped she wouldn't notice it in the backyard. I told her to put my daughter on. I wanted to hear her voice. I don't know why. She was more like me, is all I can say. They were both young and at that age you can't tell much, anyway. But she'd already hung up. She'd heard enough to know what it all meant.

I'd thrown a bottle of Gatorade in with an eighteen pack, but I set the dead weight in the garbage can out front as I turned down the street. I had a fresh pack of smokes, too. Things didn't seem that bad. I was thinking about maybe watching some late night television. Maybe getting into bed at some point and making up with the wife the way we sometimes did on these kind of nights. My buzz was gone by now. It must have been hours since my last beer. I had the whole drive home to drink beer and think about what I'd say and how I'd say it.

Down the street, I could see even in the dim mill light that the truck was gone, though there was a glint around the hole, or where I thought the hole should be, as if something was moving there. I set the case of beer down on the sidewalk and saw the hole half-filled with water. It seemed to be rising. I'd gone deeper than I thought, or at least the line was shallower than we'd thought. At some point, I'd broken it. I could see pieces of the tar-and-paper line bubbling at the surface. Somehow dirt had gotten down the line and clogged it up.

The front door was locked, but then I lifted the garage door. Water ran from every faucet and fixture throughout the house. There weren't many of them. But the house was a mess. The carpet was torn out and mattresses were spread everywhere. The bathtub had a film of dirt-red along its rim, and the water-heater had been disconnected, along with the washer and dryer, which lay on their sides in the backyard. If they'd had cabinets, those were gone too, though I couldn't see them among the other debris—a muffler, television antennae, clay pots, silverware, rugs, the refrigerator, oven. The house wasn't big, just a small two bedroom with an attic for a dormer. You see homes in this condition sometimes, where they'll position their laundry drain to shoot out their window into the neighbor's backyard, or let the walls rot down to the plaster-wire or studs. I did what anyone else would do. I shut the water off. Then I went outside and boarded the hole.

It's possible he kept driving north through Oregon and Washington and maybe even Canada, where he found a dirt road and stayed on it until it ended or he got stuck, something he'd done in the past for no apparent reason. I never asked—we only spoke a few times, generally about our pending lawsuit. I found my way to Shakespeare—somehow the whole ordeal had brought me enough sympathy from the wife to drive out and pick me up. So we managed to have a good time and make a day of it. It was a Saturday, after all. But that's another story. Who knows what I told her.

Gabrielle Idlet

Vacancies

It was ninety-three degrees the night the new neighbors moved into the empty apartment downstairs. My mother was telling lies on the phone behind the bedroom door to pay the rent. First call, she was nineteen and surfed the south beaches in her free time. Then she was fish-netted and using her black braid for a whip, doing whatever someone's wife wouldn't do. Then she was nothing, just a voice that said *Give it to me* over and over. When someone made her call him *Baby* I stopped trying to read and went outside to look in windows.

Traffic on Interstate Five sounded like heavy breathing right into my ear. I crawled along the plantings people grew to block freeway noise, and at the first bungalow with a lit room I squatted on a recycle bin and rose up.

The old guy who lived in this house scraped dishes into a sink not four feet from my face, but none of the light spilled onto me. His air conditioner whirred. There was a head-sized shadow where his naked chest bowled in. He flicked dust strands off the ceiling light with the dishrag, and when he turned away I exhaled against the glass.

Two doors down, the window was open. A circular fan fluttered newspaper sections every time it rotated. The man and woman who lived there sat apart at the ends of their couch. The woman who always wore the same sleeveless nightgown had her feet tucked between couch cushions. Blue shadows from the TV rolled over the couple's faces with the changes on the screen. A few months back I saw them naked together on the couch. Her arm hung over the side, and her hand opened and closed like a baby's.

"Hey!" A whisper made me drop backward, and a lamp went on. I sprinted around the house and down the alley until I was out of earshot.

"Hey, sneak." The new neighbor stood with the streetlight behind him. He had his hands on his hips like a superhero.

"Thanks. They heard you," I said.

The way he strolled toward me, he didn't seem worried.

"What you were doing back there is illegal," he said.

He stunk of pot. Before she changed, my mom used to get stoned with her sister.

I sniffed the air: "I wouldn't talk."

He took his hands off his hips and slumped a little, like that pose had been keeping him standing.

"I don't need to make it any harder on Debbie while she's pregnant," he said.

"Marijuana makes men sterile," I told him.

I couldn't see his expression in the dark.

"Fag," I added quietly.

"Bitch," he said, but he didn't sound mad.

I brushed some leaves off my knee. "Fuck off."

"You got a lonely hobby."

I spat on the ground. Then I ran.

"I know where you live," he called.

The next day I was stretched out on a beach towel next to the empty pool in my new and first bikini, a pink crocheted one, letting the sun brown my belly and trying to imagine the face of my father. Mom had me in the early eighties when she was doing coke. That was her explanation. So I could be the daughter of many men. Until seventh grade I thought I was actually made from my mother plus several men. I collaged my fathers, the rock star types she liked with strong jaws, teased hair and electric guitars shaped like lightning bolts, the ones off the covers of her LPs.

I was watching the dust and amoebas slide around the insides of my orange eyelids when the new neighbor squatted next to me and announced his name was Rick. He smelled like weed again, and suntan lotion, and his head blocked the sun. Blond hair glowed around the edges of his blacked-out face.

"They ever fill this thing up?" He flicked a gum wrapper into the deep end.

"I would've asked before I signed the lease," I said. Our building was only half occupied, and repairmen never came around. Toward the end of each month potential renters drove up, saw beer cans and crumpled cigarette packs and fast food bags blowing around in the courtyard and cluttering the bottom of the pool, and drove away. We stayed. Rent was cheap. Anyway, Mom just couldn't get herself to walk out the front door.

"Why'd you move here, anyway?" I asked Rick.

A drop of sweat from his face landed on my shoulder, but I didn't wipe it off.

"Magic Kingdom," he drawled. "Security."

"You're kidding me."

"What's your name?" he asked. "I told you mine."

"Asia."

"You're kidding me," he copied.

"Hey, I know it's a porn name, okay. My mom was into the band." I nodded toward the apartment.

"You live with your mom?"

"I am in high school, Rick."

He finally sat down cross-legged, and I cupped my hand over my eyes so I could see him. He had a roughed-up oval of a face, a man's face.

"Is your wife watching you?"

"She's waitressing at Denny's over there." He nodded toward the other side of the freeway, where gas stations, convenience stores, and chain restaurants clustered around the offramp. "She's not my wife," he said. "She's my girlfriend."

"Sure it's yours?" I said before he even finished the sentence. I didn't know how to erase what I said.

He chewed on his lip. Then he said, "Who the hell raised you?"

I tried to laugh like I was bored, but it came out as a weird little moan. I stood up and bent to grab my towel. He was scowling, but he was watching.

"You should move out," I told Rick. "If I could—if I were you, I would."

When I got to our door I thought I could still feel his sweat drying on my shoulder.

"It's a fucking goddamn oven in here," Mom slammed out of the bedroom. Without make-up, which she didn't wear anymore, she could have been my age. Freckles, pale lips, hair pulled back with blonde wisps falling across her shiny eyes. "Did you call the bastard or what?"

Our shitty window-mounted air conditioner was blowing warm dust into Mom's bedroom, so now she had to use our box fan, which rumbled. This was giving her problems at night because of her work as a phone sex operator. I loved that word *operator*, like she was plugging wires into sockets in the fifties. Callers had already complained that there was too much static on the line, and she was getting warnings from the service.

"The repair guys have a lot to do because of the season, because the heat makes the cooling systems go out."

"Fucking drug lords," Mom said. Her theory on why our building was empty and falling apart was that high-level coke dealers owned it as a front. She related many things to cocaine. She had been forced into rehab when my aunt and a couple of their friends did an intervention. It worked. But afterward, Mom would not leave the apartment. She said she had demons. She said to shut up, because everybody has them.

When she went back to her room I put my face against our window. Rick sat with his legs dangling over the edge of the pool. He looked like he was watching the brush next to the freeway, which shook from tankers rolling by. Or he might have been looking over the freeway toward his girlfriend. A flock of pigeons spilled off the roof and started flapping. He looked up and watched the birds, and their shadows striped him for a minute before they were gone.

Summers I read what we would be reading in Honors in the fall—this year it was Orwell, Huxley, Eliot. The library gave out the reading list in May, but a lot of people just waited for school to start back up. Most Honors students at Katella lived in gated communities nowhere near the 5 and spent their summers at arts or sports or music camps. I wasn't friends with those kids. I just watched them. I read at nutrition and lunch, I read after school and I read in the summer, and I had only one word in my mind: *Out.*

Mornings, I read with the table fan on me. Then I took the bus to the market, the check casher's, the mini-mart, the laundromat. Later in the day, Mom walked around the apartment in a t-shirt until her coffee was ready, then go back to her room. She kept another TV on in there all the time, even when she was working—I could tell from the whine it gave off when it was muted.

While Mom worked at night, I crisscrossed the side-streets between Palm and South Anaheim. Tonight, at the first ring of the cordless, I put on my sneakers and closed the front door lightly. Rick's face floated in my mind, and I had the sense that someone I couldn't see was watching me. There was nothing to see on our block or the next. Shades were down, or people were at work. I sat on the curb for a while, and then I crossed our courtyard and climbed the stairs.

Rick and Debbie's window was shut, and the air conditioner dripped onto my wrist when I lay my hand on the molding. Their unit looked exactly like ours, but reversed, with all the rooms facing the other way. She had on a loose yellow housedress and was resting a glass of orange punch or juice on her belly. He was behind her, his teeth working on his lower lip. She couldn't see how he stood so near, watching her. If I were Debbie, I would have shut off the TV. I would have turned on the couch and thrown my arms around him.

Without warning, Rick looked straight at the window, and I thought he saw me drop to the ground. I waited, but he didn't come outside. Tasting the metal of adrenaline I looked again. He was sitting beside her now, mussing her hair, and I could see from her wide laugh why he liked her. When he put his head on her chest, I stood in full view. I made a face like someone screaming, but they didn't see. There was no chance of it, from how they sat there connected.

In her room, Mom was practically yelling over the grinding fan, in the voice she saved for the end stretch. I curled and turned over and curled the other way in the wadded-up sheet on the couch. I spread my hands against my cheeks the way glowing fetuses did in fiber optic movies they ran on public television. The blood beating in my ears sounded like the thumping of a womb. "I feel you," Mom moaned. I pictured Rick climbing the stairs three at a time and kicking open the door to reach me.

We were in the triple digits and under a second-stage smog alert. First stage and we were supposed to stay inside or die early. By the pool I smoothed vegetable oil over my legs. I lifted them up so they caught a shine in the sun and I looked at Rick's dark windows. I even ran my hand up and down my calf, but he didn't come out. Eventually I fell asleep.

"Want some ice tea?" His shadow cooled my thighs and I followed him inside.

"So, what happened to your dad?" Rick called in from their kitchenette.

"I wouldn't know."

He seemed to perk up. "He out of the picture? Hey, my father left, too!"

"Crazy!" The cold apartment smelled like Freon and potpourri. I touched a hanging planter with silk ivy and it swung back and forth, and the white parts of the leaves sparkled when they passed through the sun. I saw a glass ashtray on a high shelf. "No smoking?" I asked.

"I usually just do it at night." Rick cracked an ice tray.

A beige crib in the corner was full of stuffed animals. "How far along is she?" I asked.

"Thirty-two weeks. I keep telling her to request short shifts, but she's stockpiling tips so she can take off more time when the baby comes." He brought out our glasses and sat near me on the couch.

Then he got back up to turn down the air conditioner, which was blowing out icy fog. When he sat next to me again his leg touched my leg.

"I've got reading to do," I said.

"You had to take summer school?"

"No, just—for my transcript."

We sipped and didn't talk.

"I was going to finish my Associate's," he said.

His hands lay over the crotch of his cut-offs. His knee tapped against mine.

"Asia. That's a great name. Asia."

My mother's work talk flew through my head, and I wondered what Debbie wouldn't let Rick do while she was pregnant.

Then I turned, to see if he would turn to me, and also because I wanted to. When he shifted to face me, though, I saw from his concrete shoulders and the flash in his face that he could shove me under him if he wanted. I jumped up, and he crossed his legs.

"We can be friends," Rick said fast. "Friends don't have to be the same age." He patted his hands together.

"Is that applause?" I said. I had gooseflesh.

He lifted an arm and I ducked. But he just waved his arm around.

"The other night when I saw you," he said, "I started thinking. This is terrible, what you got going."

"Oh, did you get a degree in psychology?" I said. "Oh, that's right—you didn't graduate."

"You don't know those people," he said. "You're ripping them off."

I picked up my towel. "Thanks for the tea. It tasted like dog shit."

"I'm just saying, I'm only saying," he said, but he didn't finish, and I slammed the door behind me.

Mom was waiting. "What did you do?"

"We didn't even touch," I said.

"You're down there alone with him and he's got a wife, a pregnant wife?"

She pointed up and down my body. "You, you stay inside!"

"Rick's a good man." She shut her door. "A good one," I said.

I had change from errands in wads around the house. Mom stayed in her room, and I zippered forty-eight dollars in ones and fives into the couch cushion nearest the front door. She worked that night, and I heard her, and her voice was shaky. I slept on the money and had heat dreams.

It was close to Debbie's due date, you could see. She headed out of the house in the mornings with her apron strings tucked in her pockets, her belly high and hard looking under the fabric. I watched her do that pregnant duck-walk through the courtyard, scattering sparrows on the way to her car.

Mom came out around nine.

"Are you still mad?" I asked her.

"I just can't talk to you, Asia."

She made coffee and grabbed a bag of barbecue chips out of the cabinet and then she stood near me, but she didn't look at me. There was no sound in the house. Her TV was off, even.

"I'm not doing anything with Rick," I said.

"Shut up now," she said softly, like she was saying goodnight to a child.

I watched her. She seemed like a bird that had accidentally flown inside. I kept my palm on the couch pillow. "Any weird calls last night?" I asked her.

"Pathetic." She sat down. "Guy wanted a mommy, but I mean a for-real mommy. Not even a spanking, just hugs."

"Do you ever run out of things to say?"

"Turns out I'm good at it," she said.

I didn't spend time outside anymore, except to do errands. I was up to sixty-one and coins from change. Rick wandered around the courtyard. He seemed to be introducing himself to other neighbors—the Chinese lady on the first floor that fed lawn grass to her sick cat, the truck driver who wore an Angels cap backward. Rick cupped his hand over his eyes a few different times and squinted up at our place. But I knew the sun made mirrors out of the glass. Instead of walking around at night, I lay on the couch and pictured Rick. I blocked out Mom's voice and sat close to Rick in his cooled-down apartment, and we talked like people who cared about each other.

A week later I'd run out of books. There was nothing on TV. I looked out the window while Mom nursed some poor sucker: "You need it, you know you do." Some man with a family, he was pulling her hair like the mane of a horse, I guess. He might as well be my father, needy and fat and curly-haired, bearded and mushy and skinny, quick and mean and packed into a business suit, not a rock star now, just married to someone who wouldn't do what he wanted. He didn't know how pink Mom's eyes were, or how she looked in the daylight, standing next to the couch with coffee and potato chips. "Do it," Mom cried. Then she finished him off with cooing.

She coughed, dialed. "Long legs I've got, sure. Long legs, tan," she said. "Well, I can't tell you how old I am." There was a pause. "And a bikini, sure," she told the stranger. "You know, crocheted." I couldn't swallow. "Pink."

I was up and kicking her door, kicking until she opened it, and then I had the receiver.

"Who the hell are you?" I screamed. "What's wrong with you?"

Mom tried to grab the phone out of my hand, but I threw it against the wall.

"The words just flew up in me," she whispered. "I can't explain it." I unzipped the money from the pillow and left.

In the courtyard, the heat, the exhaust, the freeway noise all batted at me until I started to break apart. My body was a billion dust specks rippling toward the freeway onramp, and the car that rumbled to a stop was Rick's.

"I know you," he said.

I got in and tilted right over against him. We drove through In-n-Out and he bought us burgers and we drove around and ate while I cried. He passed me napkins from his bag so I could blow my nose.

"I think about leaving," he said.

"You don't want to be a father?"

He parked the car. We were right next door to our building.

"I'm selfish, and I'm ashamed of it," he said.

"I'm ashamed of everything," I said.

He got out, walked around, opened my door. I stood up, shaking because it was over. But he pulled a sheet out of the truck bed and took me through the bushes at the edge of the freeway to the embankment. He spread the sheet so we could lie down.

"You don't have to work?"

"Called in sick-in-the-head."

The 5 roared. Semis flew by, and the gusts they threw our way made me feel wild, electric. I figured Rick was going to light up a joint, but he just leaned back on his elbows. He looked at me, face and body and everything.

"Come here," he said.

I shook my head.

"Come on."

I bent toward him, and he pulled the sheet edges up, so that when he held me he wasn't touching my skin.

"Nobody at school knows I live here," I said.

"You're smart," he said. "People don't worry about someone like you."

"Do not wish you were somebody no one worried about," I said.

We just lay there with the truck wakes pushing at us. "You're like something in flight," he said, finally. "I guess it's lonely either way."

Elizabeth Severn

Dumpster Digging For Daddy

I never would have lost my father if Social Services had not sent that letter requesting that I please call regarding our concerns about Reuben Stotz. I did not like the idea that social workers and police officers were expecting me to act with authority over my stubborn daddy, who had pretty much killed my mother and then begrudgingly fell by default into my care. But while mulling over the letter throughout that day, I decided to go on the offensive. Despite the 50-mile round trip, I would check on Daddy every other day. I needed to prove to myself that he was not, as the letter stated, an adult at risk. So the next day, I gave up my Saturday downtime and drove to Daddy's with a smile, straight from the smile therapy manual, you know the one that claims it takes more effort and muscles to frown than to smile, so force yourself to smile. But when I saw through the open garage doors to those trash cans chock full of garbage around which flies swarmed, that smile got wiped clear off my face. He had been burning again, too. I just knew it, could smell the sulfuric residue of his shenanigans in the air.

Inside the house, I could not get the windows opened fast enough and I got the dry heaves, which I got under control by putting my head down between my legs. A glass of water helped, too, but then I saw that the refrigerator was wide open, the shelves empty except for my dead mother's homemade jelly and some margarine. A package of warm salami sat atop the refrigerator. My eyes burned something fierce. "Daddy?"

He sat on his bed looking at pictures. "Remember Emma, Kristen? Your mother." He stroked her image. "You have her beauty. She gave you. You didn't just take it like you take so much else. She gave you that. Shit you." His stroke had confused his cussing.

I had no other recourse but to hide the evidence of my father's stupor. This is what I tried to explain to the cop later that day. Wearing Mother's pants, tennis shoes, and sweatshirt, I loaded rotten food into my car. I helped Daddy into the car and buckled him in. "It stinks," he said. "Shit you."

All the Dumpsters in town sat too close to the possibility of someone seeing me and I didn't have money to pay any fine for unlawful dumping. Out of town, I considered dumping the trash in the woods surrounding a lake. Then I considered the licorice factory Dumpsters that lined a back fence along the woods. If I took the road that forked off from the county road, I could park on the other side of the woods, haul the trash to the Dumpsters, lift the lid, toss in the two bags, and hightail it out of there. A solid plan. I drove to the edge of the woods and parked. "Stay here."

"What for?" my father asked. "Go home."

"Stay here. If you don't, we'll get caught. So stay here. I'll be right back. Understand?" He nodded. "I mean it." He waved me away.

Thorny ash slashed at my ankles as I hauled the trash. Cold muck seeped through my mother's shoes which stirred up mosquitoes to land on my cheeks and hands. I put the trash down and swatted at the bugs, pulled the collar around my face. The underbrush provided cover from detection as I crouched toward the Dumpsters. I tossed one bag over the fence. I ducked, waited, and then heaved the heavier bag up and over. The Dumpster sign warned: For use by renters only. Violators will be fined $500. I lifted the lid, hoisted the bags in, closed the lid, and hopped the fence, staying low and swatting mosquitoes on my way out of the woods.

I returned to find the car empty.

"Daddy?" I did not want to shout. I checked the backseat. "Daddy?" I scanned the woods, hoping to see Mother's blue sweater that he insisted on wearing. "Daddy!" I kicked the car. "Shit you." A cumulus cloud hung low to present a picture of Mother's face above me. "Shit you both," I said. I calmed myself and had to figure some logical path. Maybe he walked the dirt road in search of home. I could drive in that direction and find him, but then I realized that to drive meant to move the car and what if he decided to return and found the car gone? Could he have crossed over into thicker woods? A chickadee sang all happy and content as I walked the woods' edge. I cupped my mouth and screamed. "Rueben Stotz!"

I waited and watched for that damn blue sweater to come from the green woods, but the only one who appeared was the cop in her cruiser. I forced a smile and rolled down my window, the buzz of mosquitoes as irksome as the look of authority she gave me.

"Got a call about someone dumping illegally. What are you doing out here?" Debby asked.

"Riding around."

She scanned the scene, looked into my car. "Particular reason you stopped here?"

"To pick baby's breath." I nodded toward the ditch, shifted my weight, and looked away. "My father used to do that with Mother."

"Why you dressed like that?"

"I was helping Daddy clean up and—"

"Where's your father now?"

"Daddy likes the country. I'm just waiting for him to . . . you know . . ."

"No I don't know."

"You know, take a leak. He'll be right back." I pointed toward the woods from where I wished he'd just appear or she'd just disappear, either way would offer breathing room.

"I'll wait with you." And then she started to whistle. I hate that. It's so obvious when whistling is meant to irritate the other person, filled with a message to let you know you're not in charge. It's passive aggressive, that's what it is and she just kept right on whistling, some tune I didn't even know. Her intent to ride me was so obvious, I almost laughed. Then I demanded more of myself and smiled wide. Yep, forcing yourself to smile when you least feel like smiling helps you deal with stress and unhappiness. It's as if the smile muscles can trick the mind into believing it's not so bad after all. She let out a long, high note then said, "So where are the flowers then?"

"What flowers?"

"You said you stopped to pick baby's breath."

"That's right."

"Don't see any in your car and I don't see your father. If you were only after them flowers, how could your father get so far away?" She pointed toward the ditch. "I mean, there's the wildflowers. Here's the car. Hard to understand how he got out of sight."

I forced a laugh. "Yeah. But . . . " I shrugged. "He clearly isn't here."

"Clearly." She looked stern. "Your father's missing, and you can't explain it."

I wanted Daddy to shuffle his bony butt out of the woods and get this woman away from me. Then a horrible idea came to me. "What if he was abducted?"

Debby frowned. She looked way too old when she frowned. Smile my mother used to say, just smile. You look so much prettier. "Listen. You say you're hunting for wildflowers in that ditch. Or maybe you were dumping illegally. Who knows. But so. He's in the car while you're doing whatever it is you claim. Did you see anyone else around? Did a car drive down the road?"

"No."

"Then explain abduction."

Something like bee stingers pricked at my skull. "Guess it's not a sound theory."

"And what's with all them scratches and mosquito bites on your face?"

"Nasty little pricks, aren't they?"

"Pretty thick in the woods." She looked at my mother's shoes. "Them baby breath ditches muddy, are they, Kristen?"

"Gardening shoes."

"Wait here while I make a call."

"I'm not stupid. I know what you're thinking."

"What am I thinking?"

"You're thinking I did something."

"Did you?"

"Yeah. I dumped my father's trash in the factory Dumpsters. I had to hide the evidence and clean up his act to show you people that he's fine on his own. But I tell you, it was gross because he can't even shut the damn refrigerator door. Keeps having that senior van drive him to the store and he wastes it all, wastes our money. Money I could use. So I dumped it. I told him to wait here. I couldn't have been gone more than ten minutes." I hated explaining to Debby, who stood with her arms crossed against her chest. A low level memory of childhood bullying seemed alive in the shiny face of her badge. "So fine me 500 bucks. I don't care."

"Let's check it out." She didn't want to walk through the woods and told me to get into the cruiser. She put on those damn flashing lights, which attracted licorice factory workers to the windows where they took a break watching that cop and me rummage through the Dumpster. I stopped long enough to look at them and wonder which one was the snitch who called Debby the cop on me.

"These two bags," I pointed. Debby moved toward them slow and unsure like she expected to find Daddy inside. "It's his trash. Eggs, milk, cabbage, cheese. Some of his junk mail is in there, too. Some catalogs still come addressed to my mother. It's easier to bury a body than to get a dead woman's name off of catalog mailing lists. Go ahead. See for yourself."

"You want me to go through the trash?"

"That's right. To prove my story."

Debby loaded the bags into her trunk. "Let's go."

"Where?"

"The station."

"You arresting me?"

"I'm asking you to come with."

"But my father may come back to the car."

"Or he may not."

"Meaning?"

"You tell me." She turned on the engine then revved up the lights and added the siren, being the drama queen she had always been. She whistled off-key while she drove. I wanted her to shut up and to schedule an appointment for a decent haircut. I expected to see Daddy walking along the road. "Hey," I said, "Maybe someone gave him a ride home. Could you drive to his house?"

"Fair enough." She looked at me like maybe she actually felt pity. Inside Daddy's house, I ripped a sheet from Mother's stationary and wrote a note, which I taped to the door. Daddy, call the police station when you come home. PLEASE. I wrote the number as Debby dictated it.

The latex gloves she wore seemed to make her hands appear large and eager and the gauze mask covered up her ugly nature. She handed me gloves and a mask. "What for?"

"Start digging." She lifted a garbage bag from the trunk and dropped it to the city offices parking lot. "Prove it's his."

"Fine." I put on the gloves and mask then started digging for Daddy, for his sake, to get her to file a missing person's report. "Believe me now? It's his. I was getting rid of."

"Still doesn't clear up how your father disappeared. Last time we talked, you were pretty agitated. I almost hated to leave the old guy in his home with you there."

"So?"

"Impatient and irritated with an elderly person at risk."

"Yeah. So?" I crossed my arms. "Nothing abnormal about it."

She lowered her mask as if to make sure I'd hear her. "Yeah. I remember. You always were a spoiled brat." She smiled. I hated her straight, white teeth. "I remember you sashaying down the hall in your pretty new clothes all aflutter."

"You got something personal going on here against me? Trying to prove something?"

"I don't have to prove you're spoiled. Everyone knew it."

"Spoiled? I did exactly what they expected."

"Sure, until . . . Well . . . we all knew about your . . . 'problem.'" She made air quotes around the word problem.

I wanted to flee her stupidity the way I had fled Mother's accusations that I was killing my brain cells with liquor, Mother and Daddy teaming up against me, and saying that if I wanted to self-destruct, I should do it away from them as it was upsetting to witness. Now twenty years later, look what AA and fleeing to a not-far-enough-away town had gotten me? Enabler and caretaker of Daddy where Mother had left off. I just wanted Daddy to haul his bony butt home. And for just a flash, I wanted to go back to the day Mother and Daddy begged me to check myself into a treatment center near The Cities, and say Okay, no problem. Haul me in. But oh no, not me. Fleeing was easier than commitment to change and sobriety came only after Mother's death a year ago. So when I got thrust into all the concern for my father, I was still fuzzy with how to grieve and unskilled in how to care. Most days I just wanted Mother's forgiveness and on the bad days, I wanted a whiskey sour and Daddy's death. I hated myself for thinking that. I hated myself for being inept. I hated the shame. I'd call my sponsor and confess, which made my bad thoughts a little less reprehensible to me.

"I need a ride to my car," I said, not looking at Debby.

Debby heaved the trash bags into the Dumpster. "I'll assist you with that." She released the lid and let it slam. "You seem to require a lot of help." We soon were back on the back roads and there was no sign of Daddy. I got out of her car as quickly as I could. Debby leaned over and said through the open window, "Make sure you don't leave town."

I thought for sure that I'd walk inside the house and he'd be there, all confused over something, but still at least there. But no. I had gone and lost Daddy. Oh Kristen, I could hear my mother say, emphasizing the last syllable of my name as if it were a weight on her tongue. I went back outside and sat on the patio glider and forced a smile. Hadn't I done it right the last time I visited? I had left with such high hopes that he'd cooperate over the trash.

Sun had glinted off the back window of Debby's police cruiser parked in my father's driveway that day of garbage instruction. I was going to be a dutiful daughter. Debby, whom I had known since nursery school, leaned against the car's hood, arms crossed, staring at my father who sat in full sun on the patio glider. A maple tree planted too close to the house shaded the other half of the glider where it had been custom for Mother to sit. Food stains marked my father's white shorts and all but one shirt button was open exposing his thin chest to the sun. Varicose veins burdened his skinny legs. His black shoes were polished to a luster, which harkened to a time of respectable dress. He had been dapper, Mother used to say, and so handsome, too handsome for his own good. Being too handsome, she said, spoiled a man, made him believe others should kowtow to him. My father would say, Emma, to the victor goes the spoils, and whatever he had done to anger Mother disappeared with his smile and kiss.

On that day, he raised his hand in greeting. "Hello Daddy," I said then nodded toward Debby. I placed my baseball cap on my Father's head to shade his face.

"Got a problem here," she said.

"Nothing major I hope."

"Like I told you the last time. He can't burn trash, Kristen."

"Like I told you the last time, I'm trying to convince him to stop. I took his matches."

"He's dug a pit. Maybe he thinks if no one can see the fire, no one can smell the smoke. But neighbors complain."

"Don't talk about him like he's not here."

"Shit you. It's my yard." Daddy left the glider and pulled up a dandelion. "I used to make wine with these." The dandelion bloom cast yellow onto his chin.

"He's not going to be able to stay here alone." She whispered as if taking me into her confidence. "He hasn't been right since your mother's death."

"I know that!" I yelled. "I got the letter."

"Pine Haven's not such a bad place."

"Never said it was." I could tell she was trying to irritate me. I slipped out of smile therapy and I frowned. "Look," I said, "I'll find and destroy his matches. Make him understand."

"He doesn't sort his recyclables. They won't pick up unless he sorts. So he burns."

"Geeze Debby, don't you have anything else to investigate?"

"Just make sure you fill in that pit." She looked smug, ignoring my anger like she was above it. I never did like Debby and I imagined her as she had been in high school, a bossy and overweight girl with skin pocked by acne scars, a voice that traveled down the hall loud and fast. I remembered avoiding her. I remember someone brave enough had once tripped her and caused her to fall, splayed out on the cold linoleum, skirt up above her waist. "What're you smiling about?" Debby asked. The gun tucked into her holster made me realize that it was better not to screw around with a girl I used to call Dubby who now had authority and a gun.

After Debby drove away that day, I sat in the grass and watched Daddy lick his finger then rub at a stain in his shorts. I wondered why it had to be that Mother had died and not him. I then asked some power of authority who might be milling around my thoughts to forgive me for that. What good did it do?

That day I lost Daddy, I did not want to go into the house, so I sat on the glider as if I were waiting for company to come so we could all go inside and talk about the good times, waiting for Daddy to stumble down the road, waiting for night to hide my fear. I stepped into the garage where my project of hope stood neglected. My foot hit a tin can and caused it to roll across the floor. That day I had yelled at Daddy, "You have to learn to recycle." I had yelled very loudly and worried that a neighbor might have heard through the open window.

"First. Give me my lunch," he had demanded.

"No," I said. "You learn to recycle."

"Ahhhhh." My father waved his hand. "Shit you."

"I'll make labels for containers." We were in the living room, and I opened the desk drawer and found a notepad with From the desk of Emma Stotz printed along the top. I stared at a list she had written, her perfect handwriting: Pamida: jar lids and rings, flyswatter, three-way light bulbs. I tore that list from the pad and crumpled it. On four separate sheets in black letters, I wrote: TIN, ALUMINUM, GLASS, PLASTIC.

"I'm hungry."

"First this."

"Now." He stood.

I gripped his shoulder. "Just sit down. Listen for once." I rubbed his shoulder. "Just listen. Okay?"

"Lunch." He wore Mother's blue sweater that she put on at night while reading. He played with a button. "Mustard and jelly with ham."

I sniffed the sliced ham. "How old is this stuff?" I ran my finger over the top slice; it did not feel slimy. "Where's the mustard?" Daddy nodded toward the pantry where the mustard sat near the cereal. I slapped his sandwich together. "You're supposed to keep mustard in the 'fridge. You want to make yourself sick?"

"Throw it all out. Bossy." Daddy ate the sandwich, licked his fingers, and stood. "I'm napping."

"Later." I grabbed his hand and yanked him outside.

The garage smelled of fertilizer, rust, and motor oil. It had been without a car ever since the accident. "You will learn." I set wooden crates and galvanized tubs on the floor then taped labels to each one. Flies buzzed into the windowpane through which sunlight filtered onto cans and jars. "A—lum—I—num." I stressed each syllable and threw a soda can into the basket.

My father stepped back. "Burn it. It's better. Just burn it."

"This stuff doesn't burn! Pay attention." I held a soup can then dropped it into a tub. "Tin. T—I—N." I lifted a ketchup container. "Plastic—marked with 1 or a 2." I pointed to the bottom. "See the 2 in that triangle?" Daddy nodded. I suspected he nodded to get me to leave him alone. "Plastic, which will kill you if you burn it and breathe in the fumes." I threw the container into a basket. "So don't burn it again," I shouted.

"Ahhhh," he waved in my face.

"G L A S S." I lifted a jar. "You don't have to peel labels off." I threw the jar into a tub, shattering it. Daddy turned the dials of a battered radio. "They won't take it if you don't separate it." I made him stand next to me. "Plastic." I handed him a jug. Instead of placing it in the proper bin, he set it down. He fiddled with the dials then stopped and lifted a jar. "Throw that in the bin marked G—L—A—S—S."

"No!"

"Put the damn jar in there." I heard my anger echoing around me.

"No. Shit you."

"Give it."

Daddy tightened his grip. "No."

"That's it. I'm not going to play this game because I know—"

"Emma made this. It's her jelly." He pointed to the homemade label. "Emma's strawberry jam makes you smile." A bee buzzed inside the jar.

"There's a bee." I reached for the jar.

Daddy moved away. "I took sugar for her. And new lids. She needed them."

"That bee is going to sting you."

"Ahh." He waved, indicating that I was, as I had always been, a nuisance, and why did I bother coming home anyway? "Put some on toast," Daddy said.

"Okay. Some on toast." I forced lightness into my voice. I threw the jar into the tub where it busted. The bee flew up and landed on Daddy's hand. I swatted the bee to the floor and stepped on it. A red welt swelled on his hand. "It thought you were a flower."

"Ah." He waved my comment away. "Stupid."

I reminded myself that the stress—not my father—was calling me stupid.

Don't try to defend yourself against it. Let it go, Mother often said. It was harder to let it go without Mother around; she had understood the rules of recycling. And maybe Mother had understood what she was doing when she allowed Daddy to drive after his mild stroke and after he lost his license. For some reason on that particular day, she allowed him to drive. He rolled the car down an embankment near Pamida outside of town. Mother died of head injuries and internal bleeding. Sometimes I believed Mother had willed it, had purposely not fastened her seatbelt as a way to escape caring for him. Still, had Mother known she carried a death wish, she could have at least gone over the paperwork with me, given me power of attorney, put the house and all the money in my name. Could have at least said good-bye.

"I'm tired. Go home," Daddy had said that day after the recycling lesson.

I made a paste of baking soda and water to soothe the sting. "This will help." I tried to be gentle so he'd trust my command. "You can't keep burning trash."

"Bossy."

"They're not my rules."

"We used to burn. Now look. Pay for everything. They don't let me do for myself. They want to take money. Money and money."

"You can afford trash pick up. Just separate the trash from the recyclables. Then they'll haul your garbage away. You used to know this. Now just do that, would you?"

"Just. Just." Daddy scraped at a stain by a button. He licked his finger and then wiped more vigorously at the stain. Rueben Stotz, your own spit's grease, my mother would say. Eighty-three degrees and he wore that blue sweater as if it kept him from freezing, the sleeves now ragged and dirty.

"Want some tea?"

"Emma makes coffee."

"Stop talking like she's here."

"Ahhhh." He motioned me away. I then watched him walk to his bedroom.

"I'll be here when you wake up. Don't worry," I tried to be hopeful and upbeat and supportive. The marked bins would work. I just knew it.

So much for hope. By nightfall Daddy had not come home. Debby called just to make sure I was there, as if she had authorized house arrest. I wandered around the house and into the bathroom where an expired bottle of calamine lotion sat on the shelf. I dotted my face with the pink liquid. The cabinet was full of expired medicines and ointments, yellowed Band-aids, Mother's prescriptions, which I dumped into the trash. I needed to keep moving, needed to stop the images of Daddy lost and scared in the woods, terrorized by an abductor, hungry and wet and tortured. I scrubbed the sink, tub, and toilet then mopped the floor.

I swarmed through kitchen cupboards, threw out a bag of hardened marshmallows and brown sugar, bug-infested flour, and stale graham crackers. I washed shelves, jars, and spice tins and scoured the stovetop. I had lost my father just because I was too lazy to get him into a safer place to live, never took the time to help him with any of this mess after she died, leaving him with a house full of Mother, which no doubt tortured him with constant yearning for her. Spoiled, I heard Debby spit, rotten like that food you dumped. I heard Mother's voice, Ungrateful, my own voice turned on me. I swept and mopped the floor and polished the furniture. I forced myself to smile as I thought of my failing business, the calls from bill collectors. I thought of Daddy's bank account. I made myself not think of his bank account, which was not large, but was sure larger than anything I had ever been able to amass. I had not only been lazy in keeping him in that house, I had been greedy. That expensive Pine Haven would eat up any money made from selling his modest house. There would go my inheritance, cheaper to keep him at home. I made myself smile even after I surprised myself and threw the can of Pledge through the kitchen window, then told myself to clean it up, clean it up now and don't miss one damn shard and don't even think about going to the municipal liquor store for a bottle of Jack Daniels. Clean up your mess.

I worked my way out of Saturday into Sunday across the living room, dining room and through the bedrooms. After putting clean sheets on Daddy's bed, I lay down and fell asleep. In a dream, I smelled lilac bushes, underneath which I once watched Daddy make love to Mother on a spring night. Purple iris smelled like grape jelly but then grew rotten, rotten like you, some voice said and mosquitoes buzzed so thickly around me, I could not see, could not find Daddy, his face misshapen by mosquito bites. I startled awake, thought I heard his voice calling me.

I believed Daddy was dead and I would forever suffer for what I had done. I ate jelly and stale chocolate candy. I hummed a hymn from Mother's funeral. For all the saints who from their labors rest. I did not feel adequate or good enough to plan my father's funeral and fell back on the useless wish of wanting Mother to come back from the dead, but not to do it herself. This time, I wanted her there so I could help her.

The phone rang on Monday morning. "We found him." Debby's voice was perky. When I arrived in the licorice factory owner's office, I saw Daddy asleep on the couch. Someone had covered his legs and feet, put a pillow under his head. Someone had thought to be kind to Daddy. Mosquito bites dotted his face and neck, the back of his hands. "Seems he snuck in after hours through that window," Debby said. "Found the water cooler and all the licorice he wanted." Empty licorice bags lay by the couch. She bit into a licorice twist.

"I'm taking him home." I pulled the blanket off, shocked at the bug bites and scratches among the varicose veins. His socks were snagged and torn. "He'll be fine.

Traipsing around in the woods had erased the polish from his shoes. In that drab and scuffed surface of his shoe leather, I understood how I had failed Daddy. I refused to acknowledge that confusion over the everyday chore of garbage sorting had diminished my father's integrity. Labels stuck to bins may have made me feel better—see what I have done for you—but the black of those words would have cast shame onto him. Had I ever complimented him over the shine that he always had buffed into his shoes?

"I put in another call to Social Services." Debby held out a slip of paper.

"What's this?"

"Five hundred dollar fine for illegally dumping." The smile she flashed slapped my face. "Just figure it's Dubby's way to finally settle the score."

"I wasn't the only one who called you that," I defended.

"You are the only one who dumped illegally. And just so you know, odds among town folks were four to one that you had cracked far enough to do away with your daddy."

The man from Social Services plotted out Daddy's options: Pine Haven, which also offered assisted living should he need that someday. He mentioned the nursing home and home health care as well, but was pushing more for Pine Haven and I wondered if he had stock options in the place, owned by the Baptists who were getting richer and richer in town. He strongly encouraged me to contact a realtor to put the house on the market, too much for your father in his deteriorating mental health and abilities. He seemed repulsed when he looked at me, flabbergasted that I had not figured all this out on my own. "Fine. Fine," I said. "I'll consider it all." Apparently the man had heard enough about me to refrain from suggesting that I move in and act as caretaker of Daddy. Maybe he had placed a wager against me in the town's betting pool.

He finally got out of the chair and moved toward the door. "Maybe I should stay awhile," he said. "See how Mr. Stotz feels about moving."

"Maybe not."

"Perhaps you yourself have issues you'd like to discuss. Maybe I can help."

Some questions aren't worth an answer, Mother once said in response to a rude one I had asked about why she loved Daddy even though he was a self-centered narcissist. "Doubt it," I said to the man. "Don't send me any more letters, though. I don't need additional warnings."

He handed me his card. "I'll stop by in the morning, Mr. Stotz," he called to Daddy, who smiled. Pink calamine lotion dotted his face and neck. I had gone out and bought him new bottle. Didn't that prove I cared? Steam rose from his herbal tea, something the good social worker had suggested I make for Daddy. And perhaps I could do my father the favor of getting some groceries into the house, he suggested. "As I said, I'll stop by in the morning, Mr. Stotz." I wasn't sure if he repeated that as an assurance for Daddy or as a threat to me.

Daddy smiled and waved and kept waving even after the social worker disappeared. I took his hand to stop it from waving and ran my thumb along a tired vein.

You're not so different from him, Mother used to say, two peas in a pod, really.

Bonnie Roop Bowles

Gizzard Boy

Heartense has already traded off her new World of Beauty Kit for the used baby socks, cloth diapers, and butt cream. She is bound and determined to keep her baby, even if Zella and her halfcrazy daughter Adell have different plans.

Zella pokes her blackish-gray mopped head in between the doors and says "Can't you hear it grinding?"

"I do," Heartense says, practicing her wedding vows.

Zella follows her head in, barging through both doors, and pushes the coffee cups through to the rinse cycle. The kitchen is loud with spraying water and spewing steam, and the smell of baked garlic, onions, and lemon disinfectant swirl everywhere. Heartense's chapped hands work quickly over the greasy lasagna pans, as her swollen belly presses against the cool metal edge of the sink, making her want to pee.

When Heartense has dish duty, Zella pulls the pots. In the big icebox, Zella's white breath rolls as she pours gallons of tomato sauce with tiny meatballs and curled Italian sausages from bigger pots to smaller ones. She combines half-empty pans of lasagna. The puffed, dough-ball pizza crusts flatten as she pushes and pokes them together with her fat, stubby fingertips.

Hot water splashes up the front of Heartense's apron. In the region of her navel she feels a flicker, and then again a fluttering like the great-eyed wings of a butterfly. She smiles wide, opens her hands flat, massaging, cooing, making love to her wet big-in-the-belly apron. "Baby Vinny moved. He felt me spraying."

Zella stops the vigorous stacking and banging of the dirty pans. Her mouth twists, "There ain't no way. You've got gas," she sputters and spits. "You're good at laying lies."

Heartense smoothes her hands over her damp apron and then sets her shoulders back in heavy entrée-balancing posture, before going out front past the empty tables through the dark poolroom to the bathroom.

When she returns, there's a towering stack of greasy lasagna pans, sticky dough pans, and sauce-splattered pots smelling of musty oregano and basil. Zella wheels around the cutting block muttering under her breath, cussing. She hoists up on one foot and pulls the spaghetti-strainer down off the iron hooks that sway above the raw meat Adell left on the counter overnight to thaw. Zella slams it down on the butcher block and says, "Miss Gripey Gut, after you wash the pots drain the meat." The ring of the colander still hangs in the air, as the two doors swing closed behind her. She pushes her head back in, "Don't cut that sausage too long."

The sausages are long, real long—fifteen-feet of packed glistening pig intestine, coiled like a sluggish, skinless snake. The box pictures a prancing pig tipping his hat. Vinny wears a hat, a little wool cap everywhere he goes. After unfolding and positioning the sausage on the butcher block, Heartense lightly presses her fingers down the firm, cold length of the meat. She loves to run her fingers over the smooth top of his head, the soft hair over his ears, the stubble on his neck. She inserts her knife and slickly slides it down, carving the sausage into six-inch Vinny-size sections.

The chicken and beef are wrapped in oblong white packages labeled with a permanent marker. Heartense settles the colander over a deep platter and rips open the paper. The blood ping, ping, pings through the tiny metal holes.

It's different than she thought it would be, living with Zella and Adell. Heartense remembers when they'd both come to her grinning, happy after eavesdropping on her telling Vinny. Zella was quick; Adell was quicker. Before she could get the receiver back on the wall-hook, mother and daughter tooled around the corner of the empty poolroom, maneuvering between the dark pinball machines, smiling, cooing, begging, "Stay with us. Work here like you've been doing except now, your board will be free. Eat all the pizza, salad, lasagna and spaghetti you want." Both smiled with one hand on each of Heartense's slumped shoulders; Zella, short, thick-necked, and potbellied reaching up; Adell, tall, broad-shouldered, and powerful reaching down. They took turns speaking their lines like a well-rehearsed school play.

"Save money."

"Go to beauty school."

"Get yourself a little car."

Adell stepped back first, trying to set the deal. "You can even sleep in Vinny's room, in his bed."

Zella flipped her overfed face up and under Heartense's to get into her eyes, "You want Vinny to see you as a lady don't you?"

Adell bobbed her broad-face in agreement and said; "He won't see you as a piece of ignorant white trash waitress running the streets anymore."

Heartense saw things after that. She saw herself going to beauty school, carrying curlers, hairdryers and brushes around; she saw a lacy wedding dress; a new name and herself lying in Vinny's bed. She saw Zella and Adell picking and shopping through racks of tiny shirts and pants. She saw them all four, her babe in arms, attending Mass on Sunday morning dressed in clean, crisp clothes, taking communion with nothing to confess. She saw herself walking down the street, her head held up, pushing a blue stroller, everybody peeking in saying sweet baby things. She felt the weight of a shiny gold wedding band, and imagined how people would like her, and how strange ladies on the street would stop to talk to her about permanent waves, casserole recipes, gardening, and what the priest said on Sunday.

At night when she lay close to sleep she'd see herself propped up in Zella's padded chair, gliding back and forth over the polished rockers in front of the window. Zella would drape the white crocheted afghan that she'd brought Vinny home from the hospital in over little Vinny to keep the sun out of his baby eyes. Vinny would come in and see her sitting in the sun, rocking, nursing his baby, and he'd say, "I love you."

"Future," Heartense laughs out loud. She stands the half-frozen chicken on its headless neck bone, and reaches up its gaping behind. Deep under the breastbones she pulls out the heart, liver, gizzard, and kidneys wrapped with purple congested veins in one glistening clump. She pats her belly with her bloody palm, "We've got to make our own future." She sings low "Hush Little Vinny don't say a word," as she swipes the gooshy innards off her sticky fingers into a bowl, "Mommy's gonna give you a third chance."

Wiping two umber streaks down the front of her apron, she peeps back out the swinging doors to the dining room. Zella sucks hard on a thin cigar, phone pressed tight between her shoulder and ear, pulling her lips in with each draw as she hunches over the cash drawer counting every dollar, dime, nickel and penny, whispering and cackling deep in her throat, to Mickey, her bookie.

The dishwasher starts to grind again. Heartense quickly backs up and runs to the monstrous steel machine and pulls the cups from its gaping mouth of rubber flaps to dry. Then she starts through a load of salads bowls, and sprays hot soapy water into the pots to soak. She checks back out the door. Zella still has the receiver clenched between her ear and shoulder, the cigar wagging on her lip, but this time her body leans close to a pad of paper, and with a pencil she scratches through a list of team names and numbers.

At the butcher block with a tiny baby spoon, left over from when Adell and Vinny were children, Heartense delicately scrapes out the pink crumbly inside of a six-inch sausage. She fishes around and catches the rubbery chicken gizzard, the reddish purple heart, and the thin blue veins and packs them inside the empty, translucent casing. She sits a small pan on the stove and when the grease pops and sputters violently, she plops in the casing. It swells like a jellyfish. She crimps the ends closed with a fork. She scoops the sputtering, opaque bubble from the heat and lays it on the dish of blood under the colander to cool.

"Clean the pizza table!" Zella howls from the dining room, not bothering to get up. "We're closing."

The pizza table wasn't dirty, because Heartense had tossed only one pizza. The business has slowed, almost completely dropped off since Vinny was sent away. For five months, regulars have slowly stopped coming and phone orders no longer request Vinny specialties. Looking at the dusty table, Heartense feels his thick hands, talc-soft pulling at the white dough, gently stretching, molding it into the most perfect circle. She thinks of his hands tugging, the slick of olive oil, the spicy taste of oregano and garlic on his fingertips, tiny curled hair holding specks of flour, the smell of yeast rising.

Heartense lets out a light-breathless moan, then dresses the little silver pans of green peppers, onions, hamburger, and mushrooms with foil. She puts them away into the refrigerator and removes a can of condensed milk. She leaves the long shallow pan of mozzarella to be put away last. Sitting on the freezer across from the pizza table and oven, she stuffs soft thin strands of cheese into her mouth, followed by long gulps of the thick, creamy milk. The stainless steel oven door mirrors every bite. She asks her reflection, "Remember the night I told Vinny I wanted to name the baby after him? Remember when he made us a pizza with the words, 'Baby Vinny' spelt out with little diced green peppers?" She smiles at her flat, widening reflection and nods her head yes. "I remember."

After Heartense thoroughly cleans the butcher block, sweeps the floor, and puts the last dry pot swinging from its hook, she cuts off the lights and hangs up her apron on top of Vinny's. A week after they'd eaten their pizza was the last time she'd seen him. Zella and that crazyass girl of hers, Adell, made double sure of that. Heartense rechecks the oven, turns out the lights, and goes out front.

Zella is still on the phone, tapping her pencil at the tablet, muttering something so low Heartense can't make it out, but her face twists and her teeth grit so Heartense is sure it has something to do with her and her situation. Zella looks up, watching, then stops tapping and says a couple of hoarse whispers into the mouthpiece and then hangs up. "It's about time you getting done in there," she says, scratching through the teams a little harder, a little darker before pushing the pencil behind her ear. She lights a fresh cigar and narrows one eye from the smoke curling up.

"The hamburger was turning brown, so I went ahead and cooked it up," Heartense says.

Zella scratches her dry scalp, looks at her fingertips, "Don't forget, me and you are going to Doctor Wheedle's tomorrow night."

"The one who likes anchovies and onions?"

"Never mind what he likes."

"Y'all have hired a murdering shady pizza-loving-take-out doctor to peel and slice my baby from me?"

"Get away from me with that talk. Everybody knows it ain't a baby yet."

"That's not what the church says."

"How would you know about that seeing as you never go?"

"What if a take-out pizza doctor scraped Jesus from Mary?"

"Blasphemy! Blasphemy! Comparing yourself to the Holy Virgin Mary Mother of the Living God!" She gives her cigar another desperate suck, then finishes, "Anyways there was no pizza in Jesus's time."

Turning back to the kitchen Heartense speaks loud over Zella's rambling as she pushes through the swinging door, "I forgot and left the cheese out." Heartense can hear her still ranting and raving, as the door swings shut.

This wasn't their first little murdering trick. They had tried secret, less intrusive measures first. Zella had gotten a clump of green salt-smelling seaweed to push up Heartense's vagina, and stinky, chewable seaweed tablets to draw out the baby, but Heartenese crushed the seaweed and the tablets and made a facial mask. The next day her face was smooth, pretty, and bright, without one zit. That was when she decided that she no longer needed her World of Beauty Kit, and traded it to a plain-Jane mom who had a toddler. They gave her warm caster oil to drink to cause her to cramp, but she blended it with some dried rose petals, from a bouquet Vinny had sent her, and poured it into her bathwater to soften her elbows and knees. It worked.

Zella and Adell had plotted and planned on how to get Heartense away from Vinny, and to get the baby out of Heartense, ever since they both eavesdropped on the phone. Asking her to move in with them was a part of the plan to keep Vinny away. Night and day, day and night, they keep their big, black, agate eyes on her. Heartense can never see a pupil in their eyes, only a cold impenetrable blackness that runs to the core.

Opening the refrigerator, Heartense takes out the bloody bowl and pours it all—blood, liver chunks and gizzard bubble—into a plastic bag, ties it with a rubber band, and puts it in into her pocket. She stops at the pizza oven again, and winks at her gleaming reflection. Just as she comes out of the kitchen, Zella turns out the dining room lights.

During the middle of the night, Heartense creeps down the steps, staying close against the inside wall so she doesn't make one creak, and goes to the bathroom with the plastic bag. She raises the fur covered toilet lid and drops the quivering liver and veiny gizzard bubble into the water. She shakes the bag around like she's preparing Shake and Bake, and throws blood over her legs, underwear, floor, wall and commode seat.

She rinses the plastic bag clear and hides it between the rolls of toilet paper and the Virgin Mary votive candles. She'd get it tomorrow. Sitting down hard on the toilet seat she kicks off her sopping underwear and throws them sticky red into a corner. Dropping her head, watching her bloody toes, she screams. She screams for unborn babies. She screams for babies that will never be. She screams for Vinny. She screams for herself.

Adell's heavy feet plod down the hall and Zella's lighter steps catch up. Heartense hears Zella's labored breathing and her own heart pounding as they come closer. As the door jerks opens she buries her head into her bloody hands and wails, "It hurts!"

"There is a God. There is a God," Zella blubbers over and over again, grinning a white-lipped smile as she grabs their matching harvest gold monogrammed bath towels and soaks up the blood.

"Get up and let's see!" Adell says, pulling Heartense by her arm.

The color and glee fades from both their faces. Zella finds it hard to stand; she leans against the tiled wall.

Adell's lips distort and stammer, "It's, it's a little boy." The bloody gizzard bubble buoys up and down in the toilet like something alive.

"God up in heaven what are we to do?" Zella shrieks, squeezing her eyes shut and flying both outstretched arms toward the ceiling.

Adell slowly, ceremoniously puts the commode lid down so Zella can't look anymore.

"We've got to bury him, we can't just flush him," Heartense blubbers. "We need a casket to put my baby in."

Adell looks around the blood-smeared bathroom with her eyes big and wild, like there might be a baby coffin sitting amongst the toilet paper, shampoo, and soap.

"We could use a shoe box," Heartense whispers, forced and low.

Both Adell and Zella dangle their heads down wobbly and limp like they're fastened to their necks with dry rotted string.

Adell says weakly, "I'll go get a box."

"I want something soft and snuggly to wrap him up in. He's so cold and wet," Heartense cries. And then adds, "Get me something white like a christening gown."

Zella sputters out through trembling lips, "I'll go get the little white afghan I crocheted."

Adell turns back into the door and screams, "Who's gonna get him out of the water!"

Heartense slings open the blood matted furry lid, freckling Adell's face with rosy dots. "I don't want nobody's hands on him but mine and God's!" Heartense says, pointing a bloody finger to the gizzard bubble rolling over and over in the pink water.

Zella goes to her rocker and removes the draped, white afghan. Adell goes to get a big spoon. Heartense sits alone in the bathroom. She looks around at the blood-splattered walls and smeared floor and starts to cry genuine tears.

Adell comes running with a big slotted spoon and Zella follows her in fast with a Buster Brown shoebox and the little white afghan. "Is that Vinny's old shoe box, the one he keeps his baseball cards in?" Heartense says, wiping the tears from her face, pointing one finger at the box.

Zella whispers low, shaking all over, "It's the only one I could find."

Heartense takes the warped, yellowed box picturing a little boy in knickers and says, "Maybe we should use a pizza box instead."

Adell starts crying, "We can't bury him in a pizza box. It might be bad for business."

Heartense slants her eyes and says, "I guess you're right. Anyhow he might like the little Buster Brown Boy for company."

Adell hands over the slotted spoon. Heartense stoops over the commode with the spoon, stirring like it's a giant soup tureen. Zella murmurs something about last rites. Heartense gets quiet, stops stirring, then stands and screams with the spoon pointing hard, dripping on the bloody floor. "My little Baby Vinny is going to burn in Hell's hottest fire, because you're saying them after he's dead and gone! Call the priest! Call my old preacher! Call Vinny! Call somebody! she yells, falling to her knees, wrapping her arms around the toilet bowl.

Zella starts pleading, kneading her thighs, "We can't call a priest into all this."

Adell says, "He's already baptized."

"He's already baptized?" Heartense screeches. Zella and Adell don't answer. They just silently stare at the toilet bowl before dropping their heads and slumping out to wait in the hall.

Slamming the door shut after them Heartense scoops out the liver, then the sausage casing, and puts them dripping pink into the Buster Brown box. She watches the greasy pink water spiral away.

"Y'all can come in now," Heartense says, working up another cry. They both come in the door at the same time and get stuck. "We've got to put him in the ground tonight," Heartense bellows, looking at the shoebox on the counter. "Call his daddy, call Vinny!" Heartense keeps on bellowing and wiping her hands over Zella, leaving red trails down her cotton, bouquet-printed nightgown.

"Lord Jesus Christ, Mary Mother of God," Adell whispers.

"You know Vinny's in New York working with his cousins," Zella says, patting Heartense for the first time.

"Then we will just have to bury him ourselves, make our own funeral," Heartense says, "but we've got to call a priest."

"Lord have mercy," one of them whispers.

Zella wrings her hands, careens back, bumps her head against the wall and then slides to the floor. Adell pulls her hair and yells, "Mother, Mother!"

Heartense smiles and cuddles the box, pats Buster Brown and says, "I'm a mother now too." Adell looks at her through wide black watery eyes and shrieks from the room. When Zella finally comes around, Heartense stoops over, helping, grabbing. Zella screams, batting at her gore-coated arms. Heartense smiles sweetly and says, "Mom, don't go to sleep here. Let me help you."

Zella pulls up on the wall, weakly, still crying. "Where's Adell?"

Heartense goes down the narrow hall, looking. She hears incomprehensible mumbling from the hall closet. She opens the door and finds Adell huddled on her knees rocking back and forth, praying among the umbrellas and galoshes.

They all decide, although Heartense comes around much slower, that they don't need to call a priest. Heartense stands quiet for a moment watching them, clutching the box to her chest and then says, "We'll bury Baby Vinny in the flowerbed. But, we have to change clothes. It's bad enough not having a priest but we can't have a proper funeral in our nightgowns."

Adell and Zella turn around simultaneously and go straight up the stairwell, holding tight together like mismatched Siamese twins, to get their black dresses. Heartense calls up the steps, "I ain't got one. Let me borrow one of yours." Adell turns and looks back once, with tears streaming down, and nods. Heartense says to their backs, "And bring flowers to make it pretty."

They all meet solemnly in the foyer. Heartense looks like a little girl at a make-believe, tea-party birthday, clutching her box, dressed up in Adell's faded black silk dress and lace collar. The wide square-shoulders hit at her elbows; the hem sits on the floor, trailing behind her shoeless feet. Adell and Zella grip hard yellow plastic flowers that came from Adell's special ordered flower arrangement in her room, gripped so tight in their fists that their knuckles are white. They line up, Heartense in front, and march outside like a band of witches.

Blood soaks and drips through the box onto Adell's dress and the door stoop. Adell drops her plastic flowers onto the polished red drops. She fingers the rosary hanging around her neck, praying," Mary Mother of God," over and over again under her breath.

Heartense leads the march to the spot of Zella's prize-winning tulips. The moon hangs full and low over them. Its light falls slanted over the scented yard and the dusty path, as if lighting a way to the pretty garden.

"Here," Heartense says, pointing her finger, pulling a mournful face. The sweet perfumery of flowers hangs in the air.

Zella looks over the nodding heads of her yellow and lavender tulips, then to Heartense. Heartense's face puckers. Zella turns and goes to the garden shed and brings out the little green spade. She squats and then falls forward on her knees, kneeling penitent among the rows. Her square knotty hand opens and closes over the spade twice before she shuts her eyes and sinks it into the soft black dirt, turning tulips under, splitting bulbs. The spade makes a vicious, slicing sound. Zella's breath comes so ragged and deep that she could have been digging her own grave. Adell doesn't hear a thing because of her own chanting and fingering. The smell of fresh shaled earth rises and sticks in the small hair of their noses.

"The ground is so cold and wet for a baby," Heartense shudders heavily.

Zella digs faster, slinging dark webbed clots onto Adell's shoes. The thin white roots lay like tiny fingers gripping Adell's velvet toe. She screams and dances among the tulips, shaking her feet. One giant shoe goes airborne and falls with a brushy thud into the neighbor's boxwoods.

Heartense reaches down and brings a fistful of clotted grave dirt to her lips, and then puts it into her pocket. "I'm saving a little bit of something for Vinny when he comes home."

Adell's eyes roll back in her head, showing only their blind, red streaked whites. Her lips froth with foam as she keeps the chant, "Hail Mary full of grace," standing with one foot bare.

When the hole is deep enough, Zella falls back off her knees to the grass and nods to Heartense. Heartense lowers the box into the hole and says, "Ashes to ashes and dust to dust." They all cluster around the box, crying in a rising babble of unheard prayers. Heartense wedges the box, contorting it to fit. Zella crawls over to Adell, pulling up on her bare legs to stand. Each of them, Heartense leading, reaches down in silence and takes up a handful of dirt and sprinkles it over the box.

"You finish covering him. I can't," Heartense tells Adell.

Adell falls to her knees, and with her quivering hands she pulls the loose dirt over the box. Heartense plucks the remaining tulip heads from their stems and lays them on top of the grave. Overhead, a swooping mockingbird trills out what he knows of the night. Zella wails and gasps, hanging onto Heartense. Heartense pats Zella's back, looks over both their heads, and winks one knowing, tearless eye at the moon's face.

They move single file to the kitchen as if strung together in one black shadow—Zella out front this time, Heartense last. Zella makes coffee and Adell brings out a light-yellow, lemon cake and fresh bread. Heartense asks, "We're having a wake?" Heartense wasn't brought up Catholic; she doesn't know all their ways. They both look at her like they have never seen her before. "I want a rosary," she adds, "and I'm going Catholic." Adell stops cutting the cake, Zella holds the pot of coffee midair.

It is very quiet in the kitchen. Heartense lips smack as she daintily nibbles wedge after wedge of lemon cake and slice after slice of thick buttered bread. Adell and Zella don't eat one bite. They sit at the far end of the table with their fingers interlaced, palms tight together like glass praying hands over the lace tablecloth. They sit like that for at least an hour, as the sun comes up and light fills the kitchen.

Zella and Adell get up stiff and slow, patting Heartense on the head, and make their way down the hall just as Rags, Vinny's cat, comes prancing through the house, covered in dirt, with her tail and head held high. Hanging down on either side of her mouth is the sausage casing, waxen and dirt speckled, ballooning opaque blue with the gizzard bulging. Adell screams, "Mary, Mother of God! The cat is eating Baby Vinny!"

All the caterwauling and fluttering arms sends Rags slinking back out her pet door, down the hill to the woods, with Baby Vinny in her teeth.

Zella and Adell stamp their feet and shake their hands and heads, making the sign of the cross, praying out loud for God to have mercy. Both fall hard to their knees in their black dresses and soak themselves in tears.

"This is a sign!" Heartense yells, her mouth full, her fingers stretched toward heaven. "You should've let me call the priest!" Flecks of wet lemon cake spray from her mouth. "You should've let me call Vinny!"

The praying, shrieking, and burbling gets so frenzied that Heartense takes the last of the cake and starts up to Vinny's room. As she gets up the first three steps she turns and says, "I might be able to forgive you for not giving Baby Vinny a proper funeral, but I'll pray hard for your souls that God will forgive you!"

Zella closes her feverish eyes and sways from side to side. Adell rocks back and forth praying in loud hard whispers, "God love you child. Yes, God love you!"

Lying back on Vinny's bed, with the last of the lemon cake resting on her rounded stomach like a yellow half-moon on a pitch-black sky, Heartense thinks of tomorrow and how she'll talk humbly about how God gives life and how He takes it away. She'll speak of miracles and the Blessed Virgin Mary. She'll pray out loud every morning and night that God may see fit to have mercy and fill her womb again. She'll threaten confession every Saturday morning cause the sin of denying Baby Vinny a proper funeral is weighing so heavy. She'll dab at her eyes, staring back and forth at Zella and Adell, and talk about how Rags ate Baby Vinny.

A month from now, she'll tell them of the true-life story she read in a magazine at the beauty shop about a girl pregnant with two babies, and how she lost one and was still able to birth one healthy baby. She'll tell them how every little baby is a flower in God's garden. She'll tell them anything, because soon it will be too late for Doctor Wheedle. She'll call Vinny and he'll come back home.

In less than four months from now Heartense sees herself pushing a stroller down the street, neighbors ooh and aahing. They'll talk about diapers, baby stages, and feedings at night. She'll exchange recipes and talk about the latest hairstyles, gardening, and being married.

Heartense's life yawns before her. She sleeps and dreams of Beauty School, Vinny's soft floury hands, and chicken casseroles.

Hal Ackerman

Hunting and Fishing

The summer I turned fourteen I saw my mother's best friend naked. I had just come out of the woods and found her sleeping at the top of the rock garden, the one level spot alongside their cabin on Red Maple Mountain that got sunlight all afternoon. Had I been more experienced in such matters I might not have stared at her for as long as I did and run the risk of being caught; the sum total of my acquaintance with the unclothed female form to that point coming from a close study of *Playboy* magazines and the two-second glimpse of Brigitte Bardot's breast you got in the film, *And God Created Woman*.

Sylvia Zellner's breasts did not resemble Brigitte Bardot's. Her body was sturdy and functional like a building that would house the Bulgarian Ministry of Agriculture. The breasts of the centerfold women stood in the full and upright position even with their bodies at rest, and theoretical lines drawn out from their nipples ran parallel as railroad tracks. Lines drawn out from Sylvia Zellner looked more a baseball diamond, with the foul lines running underneath her armpits.

I'm sure I did nothing to startle her. I barely breathed. Yet she suddenly whirled around as if a branch had snapped. Her natural expression was always close to a scowl, and now a string of thoughts raced across her eyes that read: *Outrage. How long has he been—What kind of boy would—?* My only two choices were to disappear or apologize and I chose the more difficult.

"Sorry, Aunt Sylvia."

She put on her halter-top and looked past me down into the woods. "Where's Paul?" she said, when she saw that I was alone. There was a tone of annoyance in her voice as though I was always hiding the very next thing she needed.

"He's coming in the jeep with my dad."

"I thought you were all going fishing."

"Plans changed."

I didn't mind calling her aunt even though it was an honorary title. She was my mother's friend for a hundred years since grade school. Calling her husband *Uncle* Jack was a little weird. He was the least avuncular person you'd ever meet—suspenders, thin, reedy voice. During the rest of the year we lived in the same apartment house in Brooklyn, and he carried the pompous self-importance of a being Junior High School Assistant-Principal with him into the summer.

Paul was their son. He was a year older than me, but despite the growth hormones and everything else they tried he was still a wiry little hyperactive shrimp. He had the personality of a sniper. A ring-and-run artist. He'd kick you under the table so you'd be the one who got caught retaliating and then laugh when you got punished. If you were playing Go Fish and you asked for sevens and he had two of them, he'd give you one and then pretend to pick one on his next turn and call for them back. Somehow our parents thought we were best friends or that the forced proximity would make us best friends, which is why I was up here. Parents never seem to understand that pecking order is established on the street, and that nothing they can say about it has the slightest influence.

It was his rifle that I held under my arm now as I came out of the woods, the barrel pointing safely downward, chamber emptied, bolt thrown clear, the smell of oil and burnt gunpowder still on my hands.

"What do you mean, 'plans changed'?" she said. Aunt Sylvia was a far more commanding figure than my mother, and not just because she was taller and more physically imposing. He knew that his mother would always believe him over anyone else and that my mother would always believe anyone over me. Other mothers were always nicer to the visiting children than they were to their own. Certainly mine was. Watching her being thoughtful and considerate, granting their wishes without first making them feel ungrateful and mean for asking, rewarding their behavior, delighting in their individuality, siding with them in every dispute, all made me long to be a visitor to my own house. But not Aunt Sylvia. She adored her own son like a weird six-leaf clover, and treated me like some loud, over-sized, temporary interference in their electrical force field.

She could not take her eyes from the blotches of dark stains splattered all over the front of my shirt. She knew very well what candy stains and berry stains looked like and that these were nothing of the sort. "What do you mean plans changed?" she said. I liked how it felt to be the only person in the universe who knew exactly what had happened on the side of Red Maple Mountain that afternoon.

My father had driven up from the city earlier that morning to bring me back home, so I guess you could say it started with that. Though the original plan had been for me to stay here for two weeks, which turned into one, or actually slightly less than a week, so you could say it started with that. The problem was that there was nothing to *do*. Their house was three miles up an unpaved mountain road from the town called The Maples, which was just a gas station and General Store tucked on the side of the county two-lane, about thirty miles from Woodstock in upstate New York. The big rumor every year was that the power line was finally going to reach them and they'd be hooked up to electricity and indoor plumbing. But now it was kerosene lamps and a wood burning stove for cooking, an outdoor privy that smelled way worse than you'd even imagine, and a well with a handle you had to pump. The rubber hosing was a big favorite of the porcupines, who chewed it off to hell, and it was a constant battle to keep them away. Hence the rifle.

At home Paul and I never hung out, I was completely into sports, with a clear life plan of playing Major League ball with the Brooklyn Dodgers. Every moment revolved around baseball or some street permutation of baseball. Stickball, stoopball, punchball, running bases. I was getting chosen into games with kids a few years older. The first couple of times up, the outfielders on the other teams played in too shallow, daring the pudgy this pudgy, freckle-faced, Howdy Doody look-alike to do some damage. I loved blasting line drives over their heads. There's nothing like the feeling you get in your hands when you hit the sweet spot and seeing the expressions of peoples' faces after they've underestimated you.

Paul was into disruption. He called everyone who liked sports a pituitary case. He was always inside with his stamp collections and coin collections except when he'd occasionally ride his bike through a game in the street and swat the spaldeen away. The closest thing to athletic activity up here was trout fishing. A creek ran through the woods about fifty yards down from their house. It wasn't more than fifteen across at the widest and barely shin-deep. But there were occasional little waterfalls that created deeper pools, and Paul had discovered that each day there was one trout living in each one of those pools.

The night before our first expedition he lectured me as if we were setting off to climb Mt. Everest. How we'd have to be up at five to dig worms and that I'd have to follow him and watch every thing he did. We slept on metal cots in the A-frame attic. There was no insulation so in the daytime it was hot and airless and night it was freezing. I woke up that morning with a foot rolling across my face and Paul standing above me all dressed.

"I'm going," he said.

"Why didn't you wake me?"

"Did anybody wake me," he said with a smirk that made him sound like he was fifty.

It was cool and gray damp outside. The grass was soaking wet and you could hear the sound of the creek and a few morning birds. Paul had two rods leaning against the wall. One was a flexible fiberglass beauty with a Shakespeare reel and perfectly weighted tackle. I got the other one.

The pathway down to the creek was made up of blue slate flagstones. When you lifted each one of up you'd find little bugs and ants scurrying around in the unexpected light, and meshy hairnets of root stuff stuck to the bottom of the stone and usually a few earthworms, which we collected for bait. Paul dangled one in front of my face as a test but it didn't bother me nearly as much as he hoped.

When we got down to the creek Paul suddenly clambered up the rock overlooking the first pool and dropped his baited hook into the water. A moment later he yanked his line out and a trout sailed backwards over his head in my direction. And that's the way it was. Paul mountain-goating from rock to rock, fishing the trout out of each pool. Me struggling up each rock face to fish the empty water. I have to admit he had a lot of strength in that wiry, sinewy body. I was still built like a catcher in those days, squat with a roll of baby fat around the middle.

I sat on a dry rock on the side and let my line drift with the current. I probably got a little hypnotized trying to focus all my attention on one spot in the creek. The water was only a few inches deep but clear and cold and moving briskly. I watched it swirl around a small jagged shaped stone, a splash of sunlight catching each successive wavelet as it moved.

My baited hook had been carried some distance downstream. I stood and reeled it in to move to a better location. After a few easy turns on the ratchet I felt a heavy resistance. A flood of adrenaline ripped through the top of my scalp. I had just read Zane Grey *In The Jungle*, so I knew all about how a deep-sea fisherman lands a tarpon. I leaned back with all my weight, then quickly leaned forward and reeled in the slack. I could barely move him. I dug my heels into to the sandy creek side and tugged again with all my strength. All his resistance was suddenly gone and I was catapulted back on my ass, my elbow banging hard and my rod sent clattering down the embankment into the water.

Paul came back down when he heard the rumpus. "I got one," I said, looking around behind me, confused that I did not see it or hear its flapping. "Somewhere."

"I don't think so," he smiled, and gestured toward the creek where my severed line flapped impotently across the rock where my hook had got snagged. "You caught a rock."

"What am I supposed to do now?"

"Did you bring a spare?"

"No."

"Well. I guess you can watch."

I have to admit, the first time I really hooked one it felt like hitting a fastball flush on the sweet spot. The vibration of the strike spread through my arms like a delicious inkblot. We scaled and gutted those trout right at the stream. Slit them down the middle, throat to tail and took their insides out with our bare hands. Paul was quiet for a while and when I looked over he was crying. The fish belly he'd opened was a fertile female, full of eggs. He said we had to show more respect for Nature to throw pregnant females back in. Especially, *I* had to, he said, because the pregnant fish was the one that I had caught.

"Right. Like you could tell them apart."

He indicated some random spiral markings on the side of the fish he said was mine. He pulled all the others out and son of a bitch if mine wasn't the only one with the brown spiral. I wondered if this was ridiculous blind luck of a bluffer pulling three cards to a straight, or worse, if he was telling the truth. I was relieved when we found another belly full of eggs. He tried to say that these weren't fertilized. But when two more of his fish were pregnant he just laughed the whole thing off like he had never meant it.

It was Paul's idea to take my father fishing. He had been sucking up to him the whole morning, being polite and diplomatic like the ambassador from East Bullshit. Obviously the game was to show my father what a perfect little gentleman he was, which would subtly reinforce the premise that whatever trouble had brewed was the fault of guess who?

It was so blatant—Paul's complimenting him on things that you would never compliment my father about, like his athletic prowess. He was a CPA. The one time he was coerced into a father-son touch football game, he wore sox and sandals that made a hard flapping sound on the pavement, and couldn't run a pass pattern to save his life.

"Uncle Ted doesn't need to go fishing," Aunt Sylvia decreed.

Since my father's first heart attack when he was thirty-seven, the possibility of the next one loomed over our heads us like a safe that had been dropped put the window of a tall building—though we didn't know which floor. The best remedies doctors could prescribe were to cut down on salt and stress. I envied the horrendous bouts my friends had with their fathers. Every pulled punch and act of consideration on my part was an indictment of his weakness. Only forty years later, when a doctor looked across his desk at me after reading the biopsy results of my rectal polyp and said, "well you've got quite a bit of cancer there, Mister Axelrod," did I understand the state of constant terror my father had lived in, knowing that the elements of his mortality had been set in motion.

But then I only knew that he was being deeked by Paul, so in my most cheerfully disinterested voice I said, "Yeah let's go fishing." Paul made a big deal of saying that he'd be the guide today and that Uncle Ted should use his new rod. This was all about what had happened a couple of nights ago. Neither one of us had said anything about it, openly, but from the disgusted looks he kept throwing at me when nobody was looking, I knew he was thinking about it every second.

I don't know why I had started thinking about Paul's sister, Joanne, that night. Maybe the sheets that Aunt Sylvia had brought up to the country had been on Joanne's bed during the year and absorbed the scent of her skin, and it was like I was sleeping in her underwear drawer. Joanne was nineteen and a bit chubby, and was usually angry about that or something else. She wore sheer blouses that showed the outline of her bra and that was all I needed to think she was beautiful.

She had gotten engaged that previous winter to a guy named Elliot who was in Pharmacy school, and had decided she was staying with him down in the city for the summer. To hear Sylvia Zellner explain it to anyone at Van Der Kellen's it sounded like it had been a mutual decision easily arrived at. But I had heard some of the name-calling between them and was pretty surprised women knew those words.

In my dream I was riding double with Joanne on her bike, a red Schwinn with streamers and a basket. Joanne was on the seat and I was pressed up against her from behind, my arms around her to reach the handlebars, pumping the pedals as we rode uphill. She told me to take off her bra, and though I had never seen one before, I undid the hooks with my left hand while steering with my right. Ah yes, quite the deft magician.

The bicycle crested the hill, then began a wild descent. Joanne stood up off the seat, her skirt blowing up over her waist. Of course she was naked underneath. I could feel myself rocking against the mattress of my cot. I tried to keep the metal from creaking because Paul's cot was right alongside. The inside of my thigh got warm and sticky. I got up quietly to change my underwear. I heard his voice behind me, just one word: "Freak."

P aul delegated me the Sherpa, carrying the rods the creel, directing me to lift up the flagstones to harvest the worms. He had also brought the .22 rifle with him, which he was not allowed to take without permission and I thought of calling Aunt Sylvia's attention to it, but that would have made me too much like him.

He was carefully solicitous to go at my father's pace as he led our little expedition down to the creek. He showed "Uncle Ted" how to use the forward and backward gears on the Shakespeare reel, got him situated on the rock above the first pool and baited his hook. It was hard to watch. It was like he was diapering him.

I found a circuitous way to and jump past them like a Chinese checkers move and get to the next downstream pool first. I had never before been in the lead and it felt great and terrible to drop my line into that un-fished pool, to feel the bite and tug of that trout, to let him play knowing I had him and finally to whip it up out over my shoulder and feel it sail back behind me and hit the ground. I scampered down from the rock to the skimpy shrubbery to collect my catch.

Paul was standing there with his foot on my line as if it were my throat. "Robert," he hissed. Not Robbie or Bob like everyone always called me, but *Robert*, which only my mother called me. "I don't understand people like you," he said.

He unhooked the trout from my line and scuttled along the edge of the creek to a spot just underneath the outcrop where my father was fishing. Hidden from view, he tugged hard on my father's line and yelled, "Uncle Ted! You've got one. PULL!"

As my father jerked his line up out of the water, Paul lobbed my trout onto the embankment behind him, and then raced up after it as though it had flown there off my father's hook. To hell with them both. I circled around behind them, avoiding the outstretched green shiny leaves of poison ivy, and snaked back to the head of the creek where we had begun.

Paul thought I had not noticed where he had cached the .22 against the rounded crotch of an old red maple. The only time we had gone out target shooting he had made me absolutely swear that I would not tell a living soul. I had to say the actual words, "I swear" and then the exact thing I was swearing to.

Before he'd even let he hold the damn thing, he had to teach me the angle to the ground the barrel had to make when you were walking and where the stock rested in the crook of your arm and engaging the safety. He set a tin can on a tree stump about fifty yards away, then counted out ten bullet shells into two piles of five. He went through every aspect of loading and sighting along the barrel, being sure the range was clear, avoiding ricochet angles. He demonstrated each point by firing off another round. Some hit the can. The shots he "deliberately missed" were to teach me something. He used all five of his bullets, and then one-by-one, all of mine.

"That's it for today," he had said.

"Don't I get to take a shot?"

"We used our quota."

"We?"

He had looked at me as if Life had delegated him to express its disappointment in me and to render its decision that I was far too immature to be trusted with an adult weapon.

It was exciting now to grab a handful of live shells from the box had stashed alongside the .22. They felt heavy and dangerous in my hand, like they could change the course of the world. I put one shell in each of my four pants pockets, one in my shirt pocket, and slid one into the chamber, left the bolt open and headed down the narrow dirt road. I had to smile to myself, thinking of this moment as a movie poster: *An angry teenager in the woods with a rifle. What could possibly go wrong?*

The road up here was hard packed dirt, narrow enough so that two people could touch fingertips and also touch the waist-high stone fence that bordered each side. It was steep and slippery going downhill and I could never get the hang of hopping and gliding down the way Paul could do. He'd always look back at me with belittling contempt, as if our progress was an illustration of how evolution favored the small. But today, I was sure-footed and thoughtless and wished that somebody I knew could see me.

The hairpin turn in the trail elbowed to the right and then merged with the semi-paved road. I must have scared some animal, because there was a loud rustling in the thicket. At first peripheral glance it might have been a large rooster or a turkey. But no, that long, thin curved neck, the bridal train of tail feathers. I had never seen a peacock, but I was instantly sure that was what had just scuttled from the low thicket into the copse of slender willows.

Before my brain knew what my body intended, I had taken a stride backwards for momentum, and vaulted over the top of the stone fence, landing soft and strong with my knees coiled. I plunged down the hill in long unpremeditated leaps, holding the rifle in one hand above my head. It had been a rainy summer and the grasses almost knee high, interwoven with hidden pockets of thorny wild berry bushes. That soon gave way to thicker darker brambly woods.

The thicket was perfect terrain for the bird. There were no beaten trails. Branches of new growth whipped my face. I stopped and listened for him but he had gone to ground or flown away. I set the rifle down beside me and lay out prone on the forest floor so I could peer through the lowest lacework of twigs and underbrush. I pushed away the small sturdy root branch of a low-growing shrub. Rather than snapping off, it snapped back at me. The point of a twig stabbed me in the corner of my right eye. It felt like a carpet tack stuck in my eyeball. I howled and bolted upright, and in doing so cracked the top of my head into a sturdy overhanging bough. The impact drove me back to my knees and I thought my head had broken open and crazy captured thoughts were leaping from it that should never be let out into the world. *If I died here, would they miss me or say that it taught me a lesson?*

I brushed the palm of my hand lightly across my scalp. It was either blood or tree sap. I didn't know. I couldn't open my right eye. I had just read in Ripley's *Believe It Or Not* about a kid climbing a peach tree and getting a twig stuck in his scalp and a month later it started to sprout leaves and it sent a root structure down into his brain and he died.

I focused on being quiet, on willing my vision to clear. There was an eruption of sound from right alongside me. The bird propelled itself out of its hiding place. Its wingspan was immense and the impact of its tail feathers knocked me on my side. The rifle lay on the ground. I pulled it toward me by the end of its polished wooden stock, jammed it against my stomach and fired point blank into the air. The recoil knocked the wind out of me and it was a good thing I didn't have it between my legs.

The sound was like the world had cracked open in my ear. It surely must have reverberated across the whole mountainside. If my father and Paul hadn't noticed I was gone, this would get their attention. But most likely they had already returned to the trailhead where Paul would have seen that the .22 was gone. He might not have said anything for fear of alarming "uncle Ted," but at the sound of the shot they would have started to run. Paul would have commanded my father to wait there while he went for the jeep and my father would have obeyed. A man who fears for his life is easily dominated.

I trudged up hill out of the thicket. The pain in my eye began to dull and I could flitter it partially open. It was like looking through a honey jar but up ahead I could see the outline of trees. My bare arms were covered in nicks and scratches and I had to swat away chunky black flies that lighted on me, attracted by the scent of blood. It wasn't as easy to vault the fence from the low side. I crawled across it on my belly.

Moments later I heard the sound of the jeep's engine starting up in the distance. The sound also gave me my bearings. I had been climbing in the wrong direction. Now I righted myself and presently recognized the stone fence alongside the road. It wasn't as easy to vault the fence from the low side. I rolled across it on my belly. A jolt of pleasure surged between my legs as my erection met the return pressure of the stone. The prospect of feeling this voltage whenever I wanted to made the future look sweet.

The sound of the jeep's engine was close at hand. I imagined myself Audie Murphy in a World War II movie or Gregory Peck in *Pork Chop Hill.* The jeep was a Nazi patrol or a platoon of North Koreans and I was trapped alone behind enemy lines with only my rifle and my wits. It was strange to hear my name sung out on my father's unmusical voice as the jeep rode by. He didn't know how to play the airwaves like mothers' did calling their children home through the dusky end of day. I crouched behind the fence and let the vehicle pass. I reached back into my left rear pocket extracted the shell that resided there, slid it into the chamber and slid the bolt. I rested the barrel across the fence and sighted down the 'V'. My right eye was still blurry so I had to crane my neck across the stock and look through my left.

The hollow in the back of Paul's neck, just under the thin strap of his Yankee baseball cap was in the "V." I tilted up slightly so the single point at the tip of the barrel intersected. My index finger curled toward the trigger. I swung the barrel a few degrees to the right. And now it was the prematurely graying hair of my father's hair that I had in my crosshairs. I was positive that after firing at the bird I had engaged the safety. My finger bent more firmly around the trigger. The beveled cuticle of metal found its niche in the fleshy joint of my index finger. I felt the trigger's mechanical resistance. I popped my lips together and whispered *pow* as the jeep swung around a turn and out of sight.

The smell of exhaust was still in the air as I turned the opposite way, back up the hill. With the sun on my face, I felt tall and rawboned, and like I striding onto the diamond in Game Seven of the World Series. Look how I was holding the rifle! Swinging it easily with two hands on the barrel like it was a baseball bat. The shroud that envelops the future opened before me and I saw what I would become: A lanky six-foot-two mythic hero stepping out of one of those mythic Southern towns. Salt Lick Fish Gap, Arkansas. A kid whose legend preceded him. You heard his fastball pop before it hit the catcher's mitt. That's right. He could throw faster than the speed of sound. And that was with his off-arm. The good one approached the speed of light. And could he hit? His swing was compact and lyrical. No wasted motion. The crack of ash on horsehide at the moment of contact was biblical.

I reached the hairpin where the road veered off to the unpaved path. From the downhill side, the elbow of the turn jutted out like a parapet over the wooded valley. At the very crook of the elbow, directly in my line of sight, perched on the top level of the stone wall less that a hundred feet away from me, was a chipmunk.

I waited for it to see me and scamper away but it didn't move. Perhaps it was daring me. Like a base runner trying to deek a fielder into making an unnecessary throw so they could steal an extra base on you. I've seen the trick. I let one of the older guys try it on me. But he hadn't seen my arm. I made him think I was throwing behind him to second base. He took off for third and I nailed him (from right field!) by twenty feet. You should've seen his team get on him. And when my center field trotted by me at the end of the inning, he ruffled my hair and said "good arm, kid. Good *play*." It doesn't happen so often that somebody sees the whole thing that you did, not just the top layer.

I knelt and braced the barrel of the rifle on the wall and sighted the orange-and-black striped head. He had enough warning. He should have moved by now. I released the safety. I squeezed the trigger and fired.

A fragment of stone shot away just underneath him. His hindquarters rose up. For a moment all his weight was on his two tiny front paws. I had obviously missed him by a fraction of an inch. And that was fine with me. A warning shot across the bow. A throw to first just to keep the runner close, not to pick him off. But to my bewilderment, and growing annoyance, the chipmunk did not run away. I wondered for a moment if this was a real animal or a decoy. I took another shell out of my back pocket. I aimed and fired again. I saw this one hit. His head and frightened eyes darted in every direction. But he didn't run.

I came out of the blind and walked deliberately across the open space toward him, the rifle, now so much a part of me, at my side. I loaded the shell from my front left pocket. At point blank range now, I saw that my first shot had not missed. It had torn through his hip and crippled his back legs. That was why he hadn't run. The feeling that I had forever changed the course of the rest of my life began to engulf me. And what happened after that is like Channel 15. All snow and jagged lines and pulsations of unintelligible language.

I must have continued up the hill to the house because that was when I encountered Aunt Sylvia sunning herself. I was not aware until I saw her staring at the front of my shirt that it was splattered with blood.

"What are you doing with Paul's rifle?" she said. "Where are Paul and Uncle Ted?"

Moments later the jeep came tearing back up the hill. It careened to a stop off the path on the grass. Paul vaulted from the drivers seat straight at me and tore the rifle from my hands. "I may forgive this," he said "but I'll never forget." He frisked all my pockets and ordered me to give him all the shells I had left.

My father didn't look well. His face was whiter than it should be and I kept waiting for someone else to notice. "Why did you do it?" he said.

All I could think to say was that it had come into my field of vision. Though I might have used the words, "line of fire."

"I think you better go," Sylvia said. She was thoroughly sick of the sight of me. But Paul wasn't through with me. "What did you use to cut its tail off?" he demanded. "A rock?"

"Oh God," Sylvia's voice clogged with repulsion.

Paul took the animal out of the creche of leaves and twigs he had made for it and brandished it in my face. Its fur was ravaged. Its corpse was mottled with blood and stiffening, a look of stony blank indifference in its vacant eye.

"You knew it was alive when you butchered it didn't you?"

My father's face turned yellow, then white.

"No!" I said. It was nothing like that."

"I'm sorry, Uncle Ted, but he has to know," Paul said, like he was sacrificing something of his own. "You saw it when we got there. It was still alive."

"Daddy, I wouldn't do that. You know me."

My father's face had turned whiter and I wondered if I was watching my father die right in front of me, knowing that the last thing I told him was a lie, wishing that he believed me anyway, and feeling the hacked-off chipmunk's tail pounding blood into my shirt pocket as if it were my own heart exploding.

Contributors

Hal Ackerman is co-chair of the UCLA Graduate Screenwriting program. His book, *Write Screenplays That Sell, The Ackerman Way* has been adopted into the curricula of many leading university screenwriting programs. His prose poem "Alfalfa" appears in the 2005 anthology *I Wanna Be Sedated . . . 30 Writers on Parenting Teenagers*. His recent fiction and poetry have won prizes and appeared in *The Pinch*, the upcoming issue of *Southeast Review*, and *Words and Pictures*. His one-man play, TESTOSTERONE . . . How Prostate Cancer Made a Man of Me will open later this year.

Bonnie Roop Bowles' stories have appeared in *The Evansville Review, Puerto del Sol, The Carolina Quarterly, Apalachee Review, Clackamas Literary Review, Third Coast, Poemmemoirstory, Reed Magazine*, and others. She won the 2005 John Steinbeck Award for Short Fiction and has been nominated for a Pushcart. She grew up in the Southern Appalachian region in a trailer park with a half-Lebanese mother, which she believes qualifies her to write about outsiders, the poor, and the effects of ignorance. She holds a Master's in fiction from Hollins University and is currently completing a novel and a short story collection. She now lives in Roanoke, Virginia with her husband and two children, and their two dogs, two cats and two birds.

Theresa Boyar lives in Helena, Montana, where she is currently at work on her first novel. Her writing has appeared in several journals, including *Rattle*, the *Florida Review, SmokeLong Quarterly, Tryst, Eclectica, Stirring*, and *Wicked Alice*. A seven-time Pushcart nominee, she was also a finalist for the Katherine Anne Porter Prize for Fiction, and her story "Random Girl" was a Notable Online Story of 2003. Her poetry chapbook, *Kitchen Witch*, is forthcoming from Dancing Girl Press. Her website is www.theresaboyar.com

Katrina Denza's stories have appeared in *SmokeLong Quarterly, Lynx Eye, New Delta Review, Emrys Journal, RE:AL*, and *Cranky*, among others. Her story, "Here's My Hand, Take It," appeared in Issue 13 of STORYGLOSSIA. New stories are forthcoming from *The Jabberwock Review, The MacGuffin*, and *Parting Gifts*. Her blog is katdenza.blogspot.com She is an editor for *SmokeLong Quarterly*.

Steven Gillis is the author of the novel *The Weight of Nothing* (Brook StreetPress, 2005; finalist for both the Independent Publishers Book of the Year and ForeWord Magazine Book of the Year.) Steve's first novel, *Walter Falls*, was published in 2003 and was also named a finalist for National Book of the Year in 2003. Currently at work on a new novel, *Temporary People*, Steve's stories, articles and book reviews have appeared in over two dozen journals. A seven-time Pushcart nominee and three-time Best Of . . . Notable Stories, a collection of Steve's stories—titled *Giraffes*—will be published this fall by Atomic Quill Press. Steve teaches writing at Eastern Michigan University and is the founder of 826 Michigan— www.826michigan.org—a nonprofit mentoring and tutoring organization for public school students specializing in reading and writing and a chapter of Dave Eggers' 826Valencia. All author proceeds from Steve's writing go to his 826 Michigan foundation. Steve, in partnership with Dan Wickett, is also the founder of Dzanc Books—www.dzancbooks.org—a non-profit created to aid literary journals and publish 2 great works of novel-length fiction a year. Steve lives in Ann Arbor with his wife Mary, and children Anna and Zach.

Gabrielle Idlet's work has appeared in the *LA Weekly*, the *Indiana Review*, *Nimrod*, and *Penthouse*, among other publications. She was the first Writer in Residence at the Sundance Institute and currently lives in Brooklyn.

Christiana Langenberg teaches in the English and Women's Studies departments at Iowa State University. She was born in the Netherlands and immigrated to the U.S with her Dutch father and Italian mother. Raised trilingually in rural Nebraska, she was naturalized when she was 17. She now lives in rural Iowa with her four children. She is the winner of the 2006 Drunken Boat Panliterary Award for Fiction, 2003 Chelsea Award for Short Fiction, and her stories have been published or are forthcoming in *Glimmer Train*, *So To Speak*, *Literary Salt*, *Carve*, *Chelsea*, *Green Mountains Review*, *American Literary Review*, *Lullwater Review*, *The Blue Moon Review*, and a variety of literary formats.

Elizabeth Severn is a native of Maryland who has also lived in Minnesota and North Dakota. An award-winning writer, she has worked in many fields: reporter, columnist, assistant editor, public relations writer, copywriter, and freelance writer and editor. She is Assistant Professor and teaches various writing courses at Minnesota State University Moorhead, Moorhead, Minnesota where she is also a faculty member of the MFA Program. Her short fiction appears in *American Fiction '97*, *Carve Magazine* and has received honorable mention in *The New Millennium*. She has completed work on a memoir for which she was a recipient of a Barbara Deming/Money for

Women grant: creative non-fiction. She is at work on a novel and a short story collection.

Chris Sheehan is an MFA graduate of Saint Mary's College of California. His fiction has appeared or is forthcoming in the *Blue Earth Review*, *ZYZZYVA*, *SmokeLong Quarterly*, and *The Angler*, and has been nominated for a Pushcart Prize. He is the recipient of the Jeanine Cooney Award for Excellence in Fiction, and the Elizabeth Butler Award for Literary Excellence. He currently lives in Minnesota and is at work on a novel and collection of stories.

Kristen Tsetsi earned her MFA in 2003 from Minnesota State University Moorhead, where she saw the production of both of her one-act plays, produced by Theatre of the Invisible Guests, and the screening of her screenplay "The Fittest" at the annual Fargo Film Festival. Her freelance travel column, "On the Road," appeared for a time in *The High Plains Reader* in Fargo, North Dakota, and several of her short stories have been published in MSUM's literary journal, *Red Weather Magazine*. Her story, "Miss Neurosis," appeared in Issue 15 of STORY*GLOSSIA*, and additional stories appear online in *Edifice Wrecked*, *The Midtown Literary Review*, *Right Hand Pointing*, *Denver Syntax*, *Opium*, *Pindeldyboz*—and in print: *RE:AL* and *They Do Exist!* an Anthology of Award-Winning Short Stories. Her first novel, *Homefront* is available at pulpbits.com. Excerpts and other information can be found on her website www.kristentsetsi.com. Kristen lives in the middle of New York state with her husband and a couple of cats.